MARITIME AGENT

MARITIME AGENT

GEORGE S. COOMBS

DORRANCE PUBLISHING CO., INC.
PITTSBURGH, PENNSYLVANIA 15222

ISBN # 0-8059-6510-6

Printed in the United States of America

Fist Printing

For information or to order additional books, please write:
Dorrance Publishing Co., Inc.
701 Smithfield Street
Third Floor
Pittsburgh, Pennsylvania 15222
U.S.A.
1-800-788-7654
Or visit our web site and on-line catalog at www.dorrancepublishing.com

Dedicated to

the late Ravi Gunaratne,

a super maritime agent.

CHAPTER ONE

It was hot and humid. Upon leaving the Port of Houston, Jim Blackburn stopped at the nearest convenience store to buy a cold one. When he returned to his car he grinned as he reached for the bottle opener in the glove compartment as if he were about to do something illegal and get away with it. Jim had moved to Houston from Rhode Island and was amazed when he found out that Texas did not have an open container law. Drinking liquor while driving was perfectly acceptable. Thus he could use his imagination and pretend he was still up north, and just like in his wild teenage years, he could delve into the forbidden.

But this was 1970 and Jim was twenty-nine years old. He was also married, the father of two, and fresh out of Vietnam. Living out his youthful shenanigans was like a slap at the grown-up experiences life had shown him. Jim didn't care. The glamour of living life on the edge was still ingrained in his personality.

He had just left a filthy and oily Greek bulk carrier that he was representing as the owner's agent. The ship's holds had been inspected by the National Cargo Bureau and the Federal Grain Inspection Services three times but could not be passed for loading wheat on account of excessive rust, weevils, and faulty stability calculations. Jim knew that the ship had an inefficient crew and before it could load wheat, shore labor would have to be ordered to prepare the holds for the re-inspection by the two government agencies. A private surveyor would also have to be ordered to prepare the stability calculations since the chief mate could hardly speak English. This would involve time and money. Jim envisioned himself talking to those excitable London Greeks who owned the ship and trying to find diplomatic words to explain to them that their vessel was a piece of shit. As a maritime agent, Jim was familiar with the emotional pressures the job entailed. Sometimes he wished he could do something else but with a BA in history, his job choices were limited.

He had been a maritime agent in Providence before being shipped off to fight that stupid Asian war. He had also been married to Brittany and their two sons, Rodney and Kevin, were already born. After his service in Vietnam, Jim and Brittany chose Houston because of the ample job opportunities. Brittany found a job teaching junior high school and Jim was stuck with the maritime agent job which, albeit nerve wracking, paid well since it involved a lot of over-time. The agent had to be on board the ship when it docked and one hour prior to sailing, regardless of the time of day or night. Sometimes Brittany could not understand the hours he had to put in and that caused a lot of disagreement between them. Therefore, the joint they smoked together when the kids were asleep was not only soothing but in many cases utilized as a peace pipe.

Oftentimes Jim felt the need for sexual relief away from home and he found it by frequenting one of the whorehouses on Navigation Street. Yolanda could offer him some of the things that Brittany, with her Irish-Catholic bedroom morality, could not. Although she would never admit it, Jim felt that Brittany always adhered to the notion that because sex was a God-given urge, only the "holy" missionary position was allowed.

Tonight was Yolanda night. Jim was job-exhausted. He just left a grain elevator and knew the permeating dust and stench had invaded his clothes and body. But Yolanda would not mind. A couple of cotton balls dipped in alcohol (*para disinfectar*) to cleanse his privates would be all she needed to perform the oral sex that his wife abhorred. As usual, Yolanda smelled of cheap perfume. She once told Jim that the image she wanted to present to her clients was that of a cheap slut on Navigation Street. She had to look and act the part and her clients loved it. She even reminded them to wash their faces so they would not carry traces of their visit when they got home. Jim used his limited Spanish when he spoke to her.

"*El mismo?*" she asked.

"*Si, el mismo.*"

It took less than ten minutes to get him aroused. She had made him remove his pants and shorts to avoid any accidental spillage on his clothing. Once again Yolanda was being cautious. She needed him as a client and did not want him to get in trouble at home. Her big dark eyes were focused on the floor as she performed the erotic act he so enjoyed. She did not want to look at his eyes. Staring at the floor would show that she was being sub-servient to his desires. She was humbly doing what he paid her for.

"Now go to your *esposa* and *ninos*," she said when he gave an orgasmic gasp.

He left a twenty-dollar bill on her dresser and noticed that she had added a photo of the late President John Kennedy on the wall between the crucifix and portrait of Our Lady of Guadeloupe. Beatifying the late president seemed to be latest trend with the local Chicanos. He grinned when he thought of Yolanda's religiosity and compared it to Brittany's. But one was the Madonna and the other the slut. They could both offer him what he needed, and Jim did not feel a speck of guilt for his behavior.

2

Brittany was in bed when he made it to their two-bedroom apartment in the Montrose area. It was only 9:00 P.M. but she normally retired early since it would take her over an hour to fall asleep. She greeted him with an almost inaudible "hi" and got out of bed. There was a PBS presentation on TV with the volume on very low. She had said that the TV light flashing on her closed eyes was a means of putting her to sleep.

They sat on the bed and he tried to start a conversation about his job experiences for the day but she quickly started to recount her own. First she mentioned Judy, the single parent who lived in their complex and babysat for them to supplement her meager child support income. Judy told her that Rodney, their six-year-old, had kicked his four-year-old brother Kevin between his legs and laughed hysterically when Kevin began to cry. Judy also told her that Rodney had a tendency to pull her cat's tail and it did not bother him if the animal would scratch or bite him.

"That child feels no pain," Brittany said. "It's scary, Jim. He takes pleasure in inflicting pain but feels nothing when he receives it."

Jim reminded her that regardless of the cost, it was worth having him evaluated by a child psychologist. As in the past, Brittany demurred. She stated that he was too young to be seen by a psychologist and that they should wait and see if his behavior changed in the next year or so. After all, she was a schoolteacher and knew more about children than he did. But Jim knew the true reason that made her reluctant to have Rodney psychologically examined. He was sure the psychologist would also want to evaluate the parents and her own quirks and inhibitions would be out in the open. For instance, she was obsessive-compulsive and woke up in the middle of the night several times to make sure the alarm clock was in the "on" position. And why did it take her so long to fall asleep? Of course there was also the fact that she smoked pot even when she was pregnant with both her boys. Brittany changed the subject.

"Judy said she heard a knock on the door but there was nobody there when she opened it."

"It could just have been kids playing around."

"Jim, please listen," she pleaded. "Everybody I talk to tells me that the Montrose area is getting to be more and more dangerous. And the cops won't do a thing. They are too busy arresting gays and dope pushers. Time to move, Jim."

Jim stood up and opened the bedroom window so they could hear the shrilling sounds of jukebox music coming from a neighboring gay bar.

"Do you really want to abandon this?"

"Oh, stop being an ass."

She then told him about a new type of oven she had seen in the Sears catalog. It was called a "microwave oven" and could really shorten the cooking time. Since they had recently settled from another state, it was almost

3

impossible to get credit in Houston, and Sears was the only establishment to issue them a credit card. The microwave sold for $500 and as they were both led hectic lives, she thought it was a good investment. Now it was Jim's turn to change the subject.

"How was school today, honey?"

"It won't be long before summer break and I'm counting the days. Everything was running so smoothly for me until I encouraged my class to watch *West Side Story* on TV. I thought it would prepare them for Shakespeare and *Romeo and Juliet*. But Mildred and Sarah, the two old battle-axes I told you about, convinced Mr. Whitworth, the principal, that *West Side* was too violent for pre-teens."

"So what happened?"

"Nothing drastic. He just told me to be careful about what I tell my students to watch on TV. I promised him that next year I'll tell them to watch *Kiss Me Kate*. But, of course, there won't be a next year if we move to Conroe."

"Conroe!" Jim exclaimed. "That's in the middle of nowhere. Who said we were moving to Conroe?"

"Remember, we spoke about it the other day."

"We might have, but I'm sorry, it didn't register. Too much on my mind, I guess. There is no freeway from Conroe to downtown. It'll take me forever to drive to the office. And forever and a day when I have to drive directly to the waterfront."

"But, Jim, please think of the benefits. Their school district always has good-paying openings for teachers and the area is so much safer than Montrose. Think of our boys."

"We'll see, Brittany, we'll see. Now let's go to bed."

Jim shut the window but the sound from the gay bar could still be heard. He could identify Tom Jones singing "My Delilah" and the gays joining in like a chorus. Like Brittany, Jim had trouble falling asleep. It didn't take her too long to get out of bed. First she turned on the air conditioner, then used the toilet. When she got back, she lay down, then seconds later turned around to check the alarm clock. The light emanating from the silent television flashed on both of them. Jim wondered what it would be like to be married to Yolanda then quickly dismissed the thought for its improbability. She still knew how to satisfy his needs, though. The TV light gave Brittany's blonde hair a glow that began to arouse him. She placed her arm over his chest.

"Are you up, Jim?" she whispered.

"Yes."

"Let's smoke some pot."

They smoked a joint then made love in the missionary position.

The next morning when Jim went to work, the Full Cargo and Tanker Division of TTT Ship Agencies, Inc., was the usual bedlam. Jim could hear his Greek captain bellowing through the radio system.

"Meester Agent, when you come onboard?"

If he had owned the company, Jim felt he would have made it a policy not to give a Greek captain a walkie-talkie. They liked to gab endlessly on their little toy. Besides, they were so loud they didn't really need a walkie-talkie. All they had to do was go to the ship's upper deck and holler—the whole of Houston would have heard them. Suddenly, another Greek captain was trying to reach his agent. The two began to converse with each other, which gave Jim some respite. However the break was short-lived when he was told that London was on the line. It was the call he dreaded. Mr. Saklarides was calling about the *Yaya Sula*. Jim had found out that *yaya* meant grandmother in Greek and that the ship was named after Mr. Saklarides' grandmother Sula. Therefore he had to give the impression that he was rendering superior service to the vessel. No way was he going to tell Mr. Saklarides that his grandmother's namesake was a heap of manure.

"I received your telex," said Mr. Saklarides. "Nobody here can believe that our fleet's most efficient vessel is having such a hard time passing her inspections."

"Unfortunately, Mr. Saklarides, the government inspectors in the Port of Houston have become extremely strict since the sale of wheat to the Soviets. They want to prove to the enemy that trade with the United States is subject to rules and regulations."

"But we are not communists. Tell your Chicago gangsters that we are your ally."

"Most government inspectors are local Texans." Jim had to laugh when he said this.

He could hear the Greek captain calling him on the radio. None of the other employees in the department bothered to answer the radio call since they dreaded talking to Greek captains. Mr. Saklarides could hear the captain's voice and asked Jim to tell him to call London immediately.

"I will have to have him picked up and brought to the office to make the call," Jim said.

"Okay, okay, but don't waste time. London closes in two hours."

Captain Pavlousis was picked up by a marine transportation service and was at the TTT Ship Agencies office within half an hour. He was short, stubby, and spewed saliva when he spoke. Jim had given him the nickname of "Captain Spit." Everybody in the office had to hold in their laughter when he walked in since he looked just the way Jim had described him.

"Chicago gangsters! You are all Chicago gangsters!"

No doubt Captain Spit was echoing what his boss had told him on the telephone. Jim tried to appease him.

"Can we offer you a coffee or a soft drink, Captain Pavlousis?"

"Coffee."

"What do you take in it?"

"Coffee."

Captain Pavlousis gave him a confused look. It suddenly dawned on Jim that the captain was used to drinking Greek coffee in a demitasse, which was normally served black with sugar. Thus he was seldom asked how he liked his coffee.

Jim assisted him in calling London and took his time coming back with the coffee. He needed a few minutes to prepare himself for the discourse with Mr. Saklarides and to tell Captain Spit that the office did not store Greek coffee. The captain was still on the telephone screaming in Greek. Twenty minutes later, Jim heard him say "*Nato! Nato!*" as he passed the receiver to him. "Meester Saklarides wants to talk with you." Jim tried to remain calm and collected.

"The captain tells me," said Mr. Saklarides, "that he wants to give the crew one last chance in preparing the holds themselves. Shore labor will not be necessary."

Jim wanted to tell him that this was an error in judgment. He had seen the condition of the holds and knew there was no way the crew could prepare them for re-inspection. Time meant money in this business and the lost time resulting from a futile attempt would cost the ship's owner a hefty demurrage.

"I'm sure Captain Pavlousis knows what's best."

Jim could lie with so much sincerity.

"Fine. Let the crew do it. The ship should be ready for re-inspection at 7 A.M. tomorrow."

~ ~ ~

Around 9 A.M. the following morning, Jim received a very unusual telephone call.

"This is the Harris County Jail calling on behalf of Captain Pavlousis. Will you accept the charges?"

"Yes, yes. Of course."

Captain Spit was so agitated, he was mixing Greek with English. Jim could picture the saliva spewing from his mouth.

"I am in preeson *Skata! Ghamotti!* Those *malakia* have thrown me in preeson. I want you here immediately."

"Relax, Captain Pavlousis, let me speak to somebody there," Jim said.

He spoke to a guard and found out that Captain Spit was thrown in jail for bribing a Federal Grain inspector. The bail for letting him out was $1,500. He immediately called the marine transportation service to pay the bond and pick up the captain. He then got on the telephone with Mr. Saklarides. The ship owner was astonished.

"What is wrong with you people? It is common practice anywhere in the world to give government officials a gift."

"Not here, sir. Here you can't even give them a pack of cigarettes. It's against the law."

"Chicago gangsters, all of you. What happens to Captain Pavlousis now?"

"We will bail him out but he'd have to attend trial at a later date."

"But the ship will sail as soon as loading completes."

"If Captain Pavlousis does not appear for the trial, he will be blacklisted by immigration and have problems returning to the United States."

"Tell your people *skata nafas*. It means 'eat shit.'"

"What about the inspection, Mr. Saklarides?"

Give me a quote on shore labor. Isn't that what those thieves wanted from the beginning? I wonder what kind of a bribe your inspectors will get from the hold cleaning company?"

"I'll contact a few companies and give you their quotes on the telex," Jim said.

"And no hanky-panky on your part!" Mr. Saklarides yelled.

Jim called four different companies and found out the cost to prepare the holds for re-inspection ranged from $30,000 to $40,000. This did not include an extra approximately $500 for an independent surveyor to prepare the stability calculations and $700 to have the holds fumigated when the cleaning process was completed. The company that gave him the most expensive cleaning bid was Gulf Ship Repairs. He knew that Mr. Saklarides would not go for their $45,000 estimate. But the company was owned by two Greek-American brothers and maybe they could agree to a reduced price if they spoke to London directly. Jim called Spiro Paradissis, the oldest of the brothers.

"I'm sure you realize that there will be a lot of work involved in getting that ship cleaned and ready for re-inspection," Spiro said.

"That's why I'm calling you. I think your company is the best qualified to do the job. But the cost, Spiro—"

Spiro quickly interrupted him, "The cost is subject to discussion."

"Suppose I give you his telephone number and you can talk to Mr. Saklarides directly."

Spiro Paradissis agreed and Jim was pleased when half an hour later he received a telex from the London Greeks advising him that they had appointed Gulf Ship Repairs to prepare the *Yaya Sula* for re-inspection. All invoices were to be sent by Gulf Ship Repairs directly to them. Jim gave himself credit for his power of persuasion. This was a day of winning. Not only did he find a solution to the *Yaya Sula* boil in the ass, when he bought the latest issue *Playboy* magazine, he found out one of the letters he once wrote them had been published. He had written:

The girls of Russia and the Iron Curtain Countries, without doubt, left most of your male readers goggle-eyed. In your own words, "beauty knows no political boundaries." You ought to be congratulated for your graceful contribution to the thawing of the Cold War.

He was not going to tell Brittany about the letter. In fact, he was not even going to tell her that he read *Playboy*.

The *Yaya Sula* passed her inspections after forty-eight hours of around-the-clock shore labor. Jim felt a sense of relief and a little bit of sadistic vindication when he found out the cargo was destined for Turkey. He envisioned Captain Spit arguing with the Turks and wondered what Mr. Saklarides would be labeling them. "Chicago gangsters" would not apply and considering the animosity between the two people, a more salacious adjective would have to be employed.

The Paradissis brothers had made a killing and Jim was not surprised when he received a dinner invitation from Spiro. He wanted him and Brittany to join him at the Athens Bar and Grill on Saturday.

~ ~ ~

The Athens Bar and Grill was located on Clinton Drive across from the Port of Houston's main gate. It was one of Houston's most unique and colorful places to frequent. The music was bouzouki, performed by second-rate musicians whom the owner recruited during his yearly trips to Athens. The food was typically Greek. Mousaka, pastitsio, roast lamb, and marinated octopus were the specialties on the menu. But what gave the Athens Bar and Grill its color was the diversity in its patrons. Business executives with their bejeweled wives; sailors from around the world; prostitutes (male and female); and transvestites would all participate in the communal Greek dances. Jim even recognized a Catholic priest and two nuns (sans habits) from the International Seaman Center cheerfully joining the dancers when the band played "Never on a Sunday."

After his third glass of vinegary retsina wine, Jim felt the need to relieve himself. Spiro Paradissis followed him to the men's room. He stood in the background while Jim

used the urinal. Jim felt his kidneys were obviously weaker than Spiro's.

"There is something I want to give you," Spiro said.

Jim zipped his trousers and turned around to see Spiro handing him an envelope. He opened it a found a check made payable to him for $4,000. He was thoroughly amazed.

"What's this for, Spiro?" he asked.

"For giving me business."

"I really can't accept it. It's against company policy."

"And who will find out?"

"It might cost me my job if they did."

"Take it," said Spiro pushing the envelope in Jim's pocket. "Now let's go back to the music."

Jim felt that Brittany had noticed the stunned expression on his face. He could tell by looking inside her eyes that she was reading his mind. She started saying something but did not succeed since Spiro grabbed her by the arm and led her to the dance floor.

Jim saw them dancing to an old tango that he remembered being called "So Ends My Search for a Dream." Spiro was talking to her as he led her around the dance floor with expert tango steps. When the dance ended, he graciously put his arm around her waist and escorted her back to the table. He then sat down grinning when Brittany spoke in Jim's ear as if having a knowledge of what she was telling him.

"He told me everything," Brittany said. "You'd, be a fool if you rejected his offer."

"We'll talk about it when we go home," Jim replied.

There was a long silence on everybody's part. Spiro then broke the ice by commenting on Brittany's dancing. He stated that Jim was really lucky to have a wife who enjoyed dancing. His own wife, Helen, hated it and would always find an excuse not to accompany him to any place that offered dancing.

"She doesn't know what she's missing," said Brittany.

"It's really sad how some people have to have happiness slapped on their faces before they know the true meaning of it," Spiro replied.

He then left the table and proceeded toward the men's room. Jim thought that the retsina had finally affected him.

"How often do you get pennies from heaven?" Brittany asked.

"I don't care how you describe it. I still don't feel it's right. I will not sell my soul to the devil for a few lousy dollars."

"Why are you selling your soul to the devil?"

"He's going to want me to give him all the ships I handle that need repairs. Our company has a strict policy on kickbacks."

"They'll never find out if you're careful. Just think, Jim, we won't have to rent anymore. We can make a down payment on a house."

"In Conroe?"

"Why not?"

"With a microwave oven?"

"Yes. From Sears."

"What the fuck do I get?" Jim had to laugh.

"You already have it. A loving family."

Spiro Paradissis rejoined them.

"You know," he addressed himself to Brittany. "Your husband has been blessed with good looks and a keen mind. Yet he chooses to act like a hippie."

"Thank you, Spiro," said Brittany. "I keep telling him to shave his beard and have a haircut but he won't listen."

Jim smiled and kept silent. He read their lips and made out a few words that they were saying but the loud bouzouki music made him reluctant to join in. In a way, this situation was a blessing since the wine was bound to make him loud and defensive. Let the "holier-than-thou" teacher who thought nothing of accepting kickbacks have her tete-a-tete with the gift-bearing Greek.

The evening met its cathartic point when the band played "Zorba the Greek." The three of them stood up and joined the dancers. Jim had his left hand on Brittany's shoulder and his right hand on one of the nun's shoulder. He noticed Spiro's hand on Brittany's left shoulder. His other hand was on the shoulder of a fat whore wearing leotards. Spiro acted like he was in a state of euphoria.

When the music stopped and they got back to their seats, Jim tried to return the check to Spiro. It was a losing battle and Jim thought he would compromise by saying that he would accept the check on the condition that he could return it should he decide not to cash it. They left the restaurant at its closing time of 2 A.M.

The long drive home was made uncomfortable with Brittany talking endlessly about the check. She reminded him that he had a wife and two children and that he should show some concern about their welfare. After all, he had served in the Vietnam war and that should have made a true man out of him. But of course, he always lacked ambition and it would not surprise her if he gave the check back like a chickenshit idiot.

When they got back to the house, they found Judy lying on the living room couch. Brittany nudged her and it did not take her too long to wake up.

"He was a holy terror," Judy said between yawns. "He almost set the place on fire."

She was obviously talking about Rodney. Of the two offspring, he was the bad seed.

"Where did he get the matches?" Jim asked.

"He didn't need any," Judy replied. "I lit the burner for a cup of tea and when I wasn't looking, he burned a page from the newspaper. Thank God I was able to grab it from him and throw it in the sink."

Jim paid her for her services and thanked her for being such a saint with their incorrigible brat.

"Maybe we should give the spanking approach a try," he told Brittany after Judy left.

"You know how I feel about physical punishment. It only enhances violent tendencies in the child," she replied.

"Suppose I keep Spiro's bribe if you promise that some of the money will go toward Rodney being seen by a child psychologist."

Brittany agreed and surprised Jim by sleeping soundly all night, without even one interruption.

CHAPTER TWO

They bought a three-bedroom home in Conroe and Rodney was sent to a child psychologist, where he was diagnosed as just being too hyperactive. After the fourth session, Brittany decided to terminate the visits. She maintained it was a waste of time and money since Rodney was improving and bound to get over his problem as he grew older. The $40 per session they were paying the psychologist could be saved for a family vacation to Disneyland. Maybe Rodney would behave if they promised him that trip. Jim suspected that the psychologist was asking her questions about Rodney's home life, which she was reluctant to answer. Lately she was often bemoaning the fact that she could not be a stay-at-home mom and that Jim, on the other hand, spent a lot of time away from home because of his job. How were the boys supposed to have a male image to look up to?

Jim was especially busy at work since his company was the exclusive agency for the Soviet vessels. These ships demanded extra attention because of the intricate government regulations. Unlike most foreign vessels that prepared the required United States Customs and Immigration forms prior to docking, most Soviet ships did not have the blank forms onboard since, in most cases, they had come to the United States for the very first time. Thus, when a "first time" Soviet vessel docked, the agent had to give the captain the required forms such as the Stores List, Crew List, Master's Oath, Cargo Manifest, and Crew's Effects Declaration. The radio officer then had to type the forms, delaying the U.S. government people and the agent since the ship could not conduct business until they were cleared by Customs and Immigration. This was especially bothersome if the ship arrived in the early hours of the morning.

Then there was the question of the crew list. Under the dictates of the Soviet Union, the United States Immigration was to detain the crew (except the captain, if he had to leave the ship to conduct business) unless a crew list was sent to the State Department to be "visaed" before the vessel docked. In rare cases when the captain and most officers belonged to the Communist Party, the crew list was sent to Washington on time.

Since the Soviet Union had not foreseen the extensive trade with the West, there were not too many licensed officers who belonged to the Communist Party. Thus most of the time the captain was a non-communist, carefully watched by a commissar (or political officer) who was a communist. The commissar, who was listed on the crew list with a fictitious position such as steward or able seaman, was easily recognized because of his (or her) command of the English language. When a non-communist was captain, and this happened most of the time, the "visaed" crew list was deliberately sent to Washington after the vessel sailed so the crew was detained onboard. Sometimes the crew thought it was the Americans who were prohibiting them from going ashore so the maritime agent had to put up with looks that could kill.

Jim enjoyed working with the Soviets. The captains (communist or not) were always affable and good-natured. They used to test his drinking tolerance by offering him one Russian vodka after the other, straight, with a glass of mineral water on the side.

He never revealed to them that he had served in Vietnam so as not to alienate them. It was also against his company's policy to talk politics with the Soviet captains since it would put them in a delicate position if the commissar was present.

The *Michelangelo* was Italian-built but Soviet-owned. As was normally the practice, the Soviets retained the original name as a courtesy to the country that sold them the vessel. The ship did not have the required forms onboard. However, to Jim's surprise and relief, the Immigration inspector, Dorothy Kruger, told him that Washington had sent their office the "visaed" crew list directly. The captain, Ivor Malenchuk, had a wide grin on his face as he poured Jim and the government officials a glass of vodka. Dorothy Kruger, overweight and middle-aged, seemed to be the fastest drinker at the table and the captain kept refilling her glass till she looked inebriated. Her speech was slow but she was able to ask for somebody to carry her briefcase after she stamped the crewmembers' passports. The captain asked a crewmember to assist her to the gangway and she left the captain's office with a bottle of Stolichnaya vodka in her brief case and a crewmember helping her walk to the gangway. When she was gone, Jim mentioned to Captain Malenchuk the risk of handing out bottles to government officials. Not all of them were easy-going (or drunks) like Dorothy Kruger.

Captain Malenchuk spoke perfect English and was obviously a loyal communist since he had a Lenin badge in his lapel. He was in his late thirties with blond hair and Robert Redford good looks.

"My friend," he told Jim, "let's say we are celebrating *Apollo Soyuz*. We have Pepsi-Cola onboard made in the Soviet Union. I should have given Miss Kruger one to mix with her vodka."

"Hooray for détente," Jim replied.

"Ah, yes. We are so lucky to exist in this period of cooperation between our two countries. Our Leonid Breshnev and your Richard Nixon really make good partners."

Jim hated Nixon and had bitter memories of the war he was forced to fight. He dismissed the patriotic fervor of his fellow soldiers as a false means of assuring themselves that there was a good reason for their risking their lives. The poor bastards who perished were not heroes but moronic suckers. Of course, he did not make his apathy known to Captain Malenchuk.

"These two men are truly peacemakers."

"I always said that my people and the Americans would some day be friends. After the Second World War your country followed British advice on foreign policy. Was it not Winston Churchill who started the Cold War?"

"Indeed it was," Jim replied, recalling mental image of Churchill giving his famous "Iron Curtain" speech in Missouri. But since it was getting late, he stood up and got ready to leave.

"*Napasashok*!" the captain motioned him to remain seated. "It means 'one more for the horse.' I think your expression is 'one more for the road.'"

Captain Malenchuk opened a new bottle and poured Jim a drink.

"Bottoms up!" said Jim but he was not sure if the captain understood him.

"Tomorrow evening, I want you to join me for dinner at a very good restaurant."

"That's perfect but since we are not loading wheat until Monday, the crew and I would very much like to go to your Space Center on Sunday morning."

"I'll arrange for a bus through the International Seaman Center. I will be back onboard with the grain inspectors at 7 A.M. tomorrow then we'll talk about picking you up for dinner."

Unlike the *Yaya Sula*, the *Michelangelo* passed her inspections with no problem at all. Since he was recently handling mostly Soviet vessels, Jim did not do business with the Paradissis brothers as often as he used to. But when he came back to the office to send telexes he noticed a message on his desk to call Spiro.

"I wanted to invite you and your lovely wife Brittany to dinner and the rodeo tonight," Spiro told him.

Jim thought it was a wonderful opportunity for the Soviet captain to see a rodeo at the Astrodome so he asked Spiro if he could bring him instead of Brittany. Spiro was agreeable and they decided to meet for dinner at The Spindletop, the revolving restaurant at the Hyatt Regency.

Captain Malenchuk seemed very impressed. He could not believe how Americans kept their office lights on even after working hours. He and Spiro got along beautifully, with the Greek-American millionaire praising the Soviet system. They also talked about the Second World War. Captain Malenchuk stated that in his hometown of Kiev in the Ukraine, it was rare to find people who did not lose relatives or close friends during that tragic combat. He, himself, had lost an older brother and two cousins. Spiro sympathized and mentioned the relatives in Greece that he had lost. But when he stated that the Greeks were betrayed by the United States when it came to the question of Cyprus, the captain did not offer him any sympathy. Instead, he said, "People always have differences, so we can expect nations to disagree at times."

He then mentioned Vietnam and how it reminded him of *Gulliver's Travels*, which was widely read in his country.

"In one kingdom two people went to war because of the different ways they cracked their eggs."

"It reminds me of two South American countries going to war over a soccer match," Jim said and they all burst out laughing.

Johnny Cash was the performer at the rodeo and "A Boy Named Sue" seemed to amuse the Soviet captain. It was his first rodeo and he was absorbing every minute of it with profound enthusiasm.

Before they separated from Spiro, Jim thanked him for a lovely evening.

"I'll give you a call tomorrow," said Spiro. "I have a tremendous offer for you."

When Jim took the captain back to the ship, he was surprised to see a hospital van alongside. Two men were carrying a stretcher down the gangway with a muscular woman on it.

"It's my stewardess, Irina Harashimenko," the captain said as he hurried out of the car. He spoke to the woman in Russian as she was being taken inside the ambulance.

"She has a high fever and chills," Captain Malenchuk said. "The ship's doctor thinks it's better for her to be taken to a hospital. He thinks it's just a cold but he wants to get another opinion."

When Jim got home, Brittany was asleep. It did not take long, however, for her to wake up. Jim walked to the refrigerator for a drink of water and his footsteps must have awakened her. She stood yawning in front of him with barely opened eyes. She asked how his evening went and he fabricated a story about the thirty pages of cargo manifest he had to type at the office for an expected vessel.

The next morning, Captain Malenchuk called and told him that Irina Harashimenko had a bad case of the flu and was to be hospitalized for at least two days. She would be released before the ship sailed. However Jim was told a different story by the attending hospital doctor. The ship's doctor apparently had performed an abortion on the crewmember and she had developed an infection. Jim envisioned the poor ship's doctor being sent to Siberia.

The experience Jim had on the *Michelangelo* and his interaction with Captain Malenchuk made him think deeply about the mess that was still going on in Vietnam, with no end in sight. The Vietnamese people were basically good and the majority of them did not know the difference between communism and democracy. Did they deserve all the suffering they were going through? He decided to write a letter to the "Viewpoints" column of *The Houston Chronicle*:

President Nixon turned sixty on January 9, 1973.

Well, Happy Birthday, Richard Milhous. Of the 1318 civilians who died as a result of your recent onslaught, a large number lost their chances of reaching your venerable age.

Happy Birthday anyway.

Happy Birthday, Richard Milhous. You seek an end to such federal programs as hospital construction and care for the chronically ill in your own country so that you can divert the taxpayers' money toward destroying hospitals and maiming innocents in a faraway land.

Cheers!

Happy Birthday Richard Milhous. You also seek the death penalty for cold-blooded crimes including the bombing of a public building in our country. Need I say more?

Happy Birthday, old boy!

Happy Birthday, Richard Milhous. I hope you won't feel down in the dumps because some of your allies point an accusing finger at you. I hope you find the right defense when those stupid foreigners say that your acts epitomize an era in your country that is reeking with violence and disorder.

Happy Birthday, Richard Milhous. Just laugh it off when they tell you that you stick to diehard pretensions of manifest destinies and Patton glories. Above all, do not be swayed by the peace overtures of the Russians and the Chinese. Just bang your shoe on a United Nations table and tell the world the Cold War is still on. More power to you.

Happy Birthday, Richard Milhous, and in the interest of your obsession, many happy returns of the day!

~ ~ ~

Three days after he wrote it, the letter was published and Jim had to face the ire of Phillip McClements, the president of TTT Ship Agencies.

"You're the company's best agent but this crap has to stop!"

Phillip McClements angrily waved the newspaper at his face. He was a little man with a reddish face and a Scottish temper.

"Why don't you show some patriotism for the country you fought for instead of bad-mouthing the president?" he growled.

"I fought for a democracy that permits freedom of speech," Jim replied.

He knew that Phillip McClements's bark was bigger than his bite. As president of a maritime company he was compelled to flaunt the redneck mentality of the industry. Furthermore, he, too, would soon be celebrating the big six-oh and nearing retirement, so the letter Jim had written probably struck a sensitive cord and gave him the old-age jitters.

"The trouble with you young hippie-types is that you think you can change the world by just screaming. But read my lips, son, you'll mellow down when you get to be my age."

They were interrupted by Jane, the secretary in Jim's department, advising him that there was somebody to see him.

"Fidelity, bravery, integrity," she whispered, then placed her right index finger on her lips as if she had just told him a secret.

"I'm sorry, Mr. McClements," Jim told his boss. "I have a Soviet ship in port and the FBI is here to see me."

"HA!" roared Phillip McClements. "Make sure you show him your letter."

Ron Fabri was not your stereotypical FBI agent. He was short and soft-spoken. His fumbling, insecure manner reminded Jim of Inspector Clouseau with a southern drawl. He wanted to know about the *Michelangelo*. The vessel had obviously been closely watched since he knew that the crewmembers had gone ashore. He asked Jim a number of questions, speaking slowly as if to allow him to think before answering.

"Did the captain ask you for maps of the city?"

"No, sir, he didn't."

"Did he go ashore?"

"Yes, sir, he did. I took him ashore myself."

"Where did you go?"

"Dinner at The Spindletop and then the rodeo."

"Is any of the cargo destined for Cuba?"

Jim paused before answering. The cargo was manifested for Novorossiysk in the Soviet Union but since the ship was not scheduled to receive provisions nor fuel or diesel Jim reckoned that a stopover in Havana was likely to take place.

Aloud he said, "You know about the trade ban to Cuba as well as I do. U.S. Customs would seize the cargo if they found out some of it was to be discharged in Cuba."

"I don't trust those Ruskies," Ron Fabri said.

"Does anybody trust the Ruskies?" asked Jim, hoping he'd leave since he had a lot of work to do.

There was a telephone call for him. It was Spiro Paradissis. Jim said he would call him back later. He felt uncomfortable with the ears of the FBI listening to him talking on the telephone. After half and hour, which seemed to last an eternity, Ron Fabri left and Jim called Spiro Paradissis.

"My brother Mario and I wish to meet with you," Spiro said. "Do you think you can spare some time from the office and drive here?"

Jim told him he could do it during his lunch break.

"Good, I'll order us some gyros sandwiches."

Jim drove by Yolanda's whorehouse on Navigation Street on his way to Gulf Ship Repairs and wished he had time for a quickie. He was, however, too anxious to know what the Paradissis brothers had in mind. Surely, they were not going to give him another kickback since he hadn't dealt with them in a long time.

Spiro was more outdoing than his younger brother so Jim expected him to do most of the talking.

"We want you to work for us," he told Jim.

Jim was stunned. "I don't know a thing about ship repairs or hold cleaning," he said.

"But you know about being a super maritime agent."

Spiro went on to explain that they were going to open their own maritime agency. They were hoping to obtain the Soviet account by offering them a low agency fee. They would both be leaving for Moscow next week and hoped to influence Sovinflot to use them as agents. Of course they had a better chance of getting the account if they hired Jim since the Soviets were familiar with his excellent service.

"What would you expect as a salary?" Spiro asked him.

Jim was honest and told him that with the overtime he averaged $30,000 per year.

"We are willing to guarantee you a yearly salary of $40,000. We will also lease you a car, pay for your gas, and give you an entertainment allowance. After all, we wish to keep the Soviet captains happy."

Jim also found out that the "amazing" Paradissis brothers had other pans on the fire. In addition to Moscow they planned to visit Athens and London to make contact with the prominent names in the chemical tankers trade. They were name-dropping left and right: Onassis, Niarchos, Colocotronis, and a plethora of other Greek tanker owners. In fact, Spiro and Mario were intending on becoming ship owners themselves. The molasses and vegetable oil export trade was expanding between the United States and Latin America and they were thinking of purchasing a small vessel for that purpose.

Jim knew that this was an offer he had to accept but decided not to commit himself for the time being. He told them he would give them a call after he spoke to Brittany.

When he got home, however, he found out that Spiro had beaten him to the draw and had already spoken to Brittany. She mentioned it to him nonchalantly after she recounted the tough day she had at school and the usual complaints about Rodney's behavior. If Jim accepted the offer, they might be able to afford her becoming a part-time substitute teacher and that way she could spend more time at home. After all, the boys (especially Rodney) would benefit by having her stay home more often.

CHAPTER THREE

The Houston Chronicle
May 2, 1973
"Viewpoints"

Submitted by Jim Blackburn:

> The reporter, Margaret Laing, who explored the sex life of British Prime Minister Edward Heath should thank her lucky stars that she found him to be overly innocent in sexual matters.
>
> Had she come to the United States and decided to write a similar report about Henry Kissinger or Ted Kennedy, she probably would have died of overexhaustion or other causes.

Although Jim was a Democrat and had idolized John and Robert Kennedy, he developed a certain apathy toward Teddy and Jackie—Teddy for his obvious lying and Jackie because of her materialistic ways.

He refused to acknowledge the fact that he, too, was now leaning toward the material world. As operations manager of the newly formed Gulf Coast Ship Agencies, he had gotten rid of his hippie appearance and when he had no ships in port, he showed up at the office in his new $200 suits.

The Paradissis brothers were busy with their other ventures. They had bought their molasses carrier, the MT *Mavrodaphne* and focused their attention primarily on the booking of cargo. They hired new staff to manage the ship repair company and entrusted the agency operation to Jim. Jim still went to ships but was using two young men he had employed to do a lot of the legwork.

Sandra O'Hara was twenty-two, petite, and with a penchant for western wear. Her green eyes and red hair revealed her Irish roots. Jim hired her because she was an excellent typist and he needed help for the extensive documentation involved in the maritime trade. Sandra was born and raised in Big Timber, Montana. After her freshman year at Rocky Mountain College, her boyfriend, Mark Perriman, talked her into joining him in Houston when he found a job there as a garage mechanic. Sandra seemed to regret the fact that she had put a hold on her college education and Jim sensed that she was harboring some regrets for leaving her Big Sky haven to follow Mark.

"That Houston humidity is atrocious," she told Jim. "Look how frizzy my hair is getting."

Jim felt her hair and the static made them both laugh. Although mini-skirts were becoming out of style, he appreciated the fact that she still wore them in denim and wide pockets to match her cowgirl blouses. It was quite a refreshing contrast to the pantsuits that Brittany wore at her part-time teaching job. Jim would sometimes stare at Sandra as if mesmerized by her small-town charm. She would smile to reassure him that it did not bother her. She was neither a flirt nor a tease. She was just a good ol' girl from Montana.

Brittany had met Sandra soon after she was hired. Jim knew that Brittany often spoke to Spiro's wife Helen on the telephone and he did not want her to draw the wrong conclusions by hiding his attractive assistant from her.

The three met for Mexican dinner one night after work. Mark had chosen not to join them. Brittany kept flaunting her intellect by giving her interpretation of popular contemporary novels and movies. Of course, few people realized that *Who's Afraid of Virginia Woolf* was really the story of two latent homosexual men married to two latent lesbians.

"Oh, so that's what it was," said Sandra. "Thanks for telling me. Me and my boyfriend couldn't figure it out. Damn good acting, though."

"For sure," Brittany agreed, "I think both Liz and Burton deserve Oscar nominations."

"And Liz should get a special award for all the weight she gained for that role."

Jim tried not partake in the female chitchat. He kept silent most of the evening as if allowing the two women to get to know each other. When the evening ended, Brittany gave Sandra a big hug. On the way home she told Jim she liked his new assistant even though she had a poor sense of fashion.

Three months after she got hired, Sandra faced her first big challenge as Jim's assistant. The MT *Aegean Sun*, a tanker, sailed from Houston after discharging a cargo of crude oil then went aground upon dropping the Houston pilot at the Galveston sea buoy in international waters. Luckily the United States Coast Guard rescued the crew and took them to local hospitals. As the ship's agent, Jim had to communicate with the ship's owners, the insurance company, the Coast Guard, and St. Mary's hospital, where the crew was taken. The telephone rang ceaselessly and Sandra had to put several calls on hold or take messages as Jim frantically answered one call at a time. Robert and Joe, the two agents he had hired, were busy handling other ships so the *Aegean Sun* was strictly Jim's responsibility.

As perspiration descended from his forehead to his chin, he found a few seconds to thank Sandra for the help she was giving him. Since she had brown-bagged her lunch, she offered to share it with him so they could both be available to answer the telephone. The *Aegean Sun* did not completely sink and the owners procrastinated before making arrangements to have the ship salvaged. That was a serious error on their part since after the ship was in a tilted position for a day and a half, Captain Ralph Tulley, the owner of a local launch company, sent his son and other staff members onboard to not only salvage the abandoned ship but also claim possession of it under international laws of the sea. Both Houston newspapers seemed to applaud the courage of the Tulley group, notwithstanding the fact that they were modern-day pirates. Jim foresaw a trial in the offing and hoped it would not be held in Houston, where he was bound to be involved. Fortunately, it was agreed that the matter would be settled in the Hague and the owners were allowed to retrieve their ship and have it sent to Todd Shipyards in Galveston with tug assistance for repairs.

Jim, Sandra, Robert, and Joe all went for cocktails to celebrate the end of the nerve-wracking ordeal. Jim kissed Sandra on the lips before escorting her to her car. He tried to make it a long, passionate kiss but she gently released herself from him.

For the next few days, Sandra kept shrugging off Jim's advances in her usual good-natured manner. She always made him feel as though she was flattered that he found her attractive.

"You're just a tease," he would tell her jokingly.

"And you're a married man who knows how to lure a woman."

Jim wondered why she and Mark never married but he did not venture to ask her. He did not want to talk about Mark Perriman since he might reveal to her the traces of envy concealed inside of him.

Sandra, on the other hand, never mentioned her boyfriend but would often inquire about Brittany and the boys. Jim spoke freely about Brittany's obsessive-compulsive ways and Rodney's belligerent behavior. Sandra was a good listener but she never offered him any advice. She had an unspoken agreement with him that she would not be judgmental of his wife, but he always felt a sense of relief by getting it off his chest.

Brittany sometimes used to surprise them by unexpectedly showing up at the office with Rodney and Kevin and Sandra always greeted her with a hug. It took over four years before Brittany was able to fulfill her promise to the boys about going to Disneyland. Every summer Jim would procrastinate because of his busy schedule. Brittany finally told him that she was determined to go with the boys even if he was too busy to join them. She chose the newly opened Disney World in Florida instead of Disneyland since the airfare from Houston was cheaper. They planned on being away for ten days.

Jim welcomed his temporary bachelor status. Sandra also took a couple of days off, stating that she had to attend to certain matters at home. When she returned, Jim noticed she wore excessive make-up especially under her left eye, as if she were trying to conceal a shiner. He did not mention it to her since he did not want to embarrass her. Sandra answered the telephone and when Jim noticed the tears streaming down her face, he guessed that it was Mark who was calling her.

"Why don't you move!" she screamed. "Get the fuck out of my life!"

She slammed the receiver and Jim could not help but ask her what was the matter.

"He's too good for his own good," she replied.

Jim was baffled. "So good and he beats you up?"

"That was the first time he ever laid a finger on me. In many ways I had it coming to me. I razz him because he is too much of a 'Jesus freak.' If he followed only one denomination, it wouldn't have been that bad."

She went on to explain that Mark was obsessed with the whole concept of Christianity and attended several Christian services. He would spend hours reading the Bible or watching the televangelists on the boob tube. It had also affected his pocketbook since a great part of his salary went to church donations. He would even donate money to Jewish synagogues to support the state of Israel. After all, the Old Testament clearly indicated that all Jews were to return to Israel and eventually become Christians. Sandra seemed to be at the end of her rope.

"Have you ever thought of leaving him?" Jim asked.

"I still love him."

The conversation continued after they went out for drinks. Sandra nervously lit one cigarette after another.

"You should look at yourself in the mirror," Jim told her. "You're much too young and beautiful to be going through this kind of hell."

After her third Bloody Mary, Sandra surprised Jim by asking him to take her to his home.

"I'd like to teach that bastard a lesson," she said.

"What if he becomes violent again?"

"I'll cross that bridge when I get there. Please Jim, take me to your place."

When they were inside his red Dodge, Jim stared at her as if giving her a chance to change her mind. She did not say a word but instead unbuttoned her blouse and exposed her breasts. The racket caused by drunks leaving the bar made Jim drive to another parking lot, which seemed completely empty. He kissed her tenderly and asked her to join him in the back seat. Sandra removed her brassiere and Jim kissed and sucked her nipples until they were stone hard. His laboring lips whispered, "You're gorgeous." It took a few minutes for them to be completely naked and they both screamed during their orgasms. Jim was thirty-four but felt like seventeen-years-old, losing his virginity in a Cranston, Rhode Island, empty parking lot "way back when."

He took her to his home and she mentioned that she preferred not to sleep or make love in the master bedroom. They made love on the living-room couch. It opened into a bed and that was where they spent the night.

The next morning, Sandra called Mark from work. Robert and Joe were on ships so she was able to scream.

"Yes, I did have a fling last night," Jim heard her say.

The telephone conversation lasted over twenty minutes. This time, however, there were no tears streaming down her face. She seemed to be in an attacking mood and words like "loser," "religious nut," and "hallelujah freak" came out of her mouth repetitively.

She slammed the receiver after she said, "Say a prayer for me next time you see Oral Roberts. Pray for my redemption."

She walked inside Jim's office.

"I'm going to have to find another place," she said. "The lease is in his name but I bought most of the furniture."

"Kiss the furniture goodbye and get him out of your life," Jim replied. "It's worth it. I'll help you all I can."

"Do you love me, Jim?"

"Yes. I fell for you the day you applied for the job."

"How about Brittany and the boys?"

"I'm devoted to my sons but have lost any romantic love I had for Brittany."

"What are we going to do?"

"Give it time, Sandra. Please, please give it time."

It did not take a long time. Six months to be exact. One thing about a paranoiac mind is that sometimes it hits the jackpot. Brittany became suspicious when he spent long hours away from home. He, of course, blamed it on work.

Brittany even attempted to turn Sandra into her confidante. She would often call her and ask her how busy they were and how many ships they had in port. Jim used to give Sandra the names of fictitious ships and invented ETAs. Sandra told Jim Brittany probably knew she was not telling her the truth by the tone of her voice. She was never a good liar. Neither Sandra nor Jim knew that Brittany had hired a private detective to follow them.

Sandra had moved to a furnished one-bedroom apartment with Jim absorbing the rent. He often used to spend an extended lunch hour by going to Sandra's apartment. They left the office separately and returned separately so Joe and Robert would not get suspicious. They had no idea that the private detective was following them.

When Brittany was made aware of what was going on, she decided to show up at the office with the boys. Robert told Brittany that as far as he knew, Jim had gone out for lunch. Brittany decided to wait for him. Kevin wanted a drink and Robert went to the refrigerator to get some sodas. He returned with the drinks as well as the lunch that Brittany had brown-bagged for Jim.

"If y'all are hungry," he said, "I'm sure Jim won't mind."

Brittany gave him a look that could kill.

It took a good hour and a half for Jim to return. He looked surprised to see Brittany. He asked Robert if there were any messages for him.

Before Robert could reply, Brittany said, "Your conscience called to say you're a son of a bitch."

Jim gave her a stern look but did not answer. He walked to his office and she followed him, closing the door behind her.

"How long has this been going on?" she asked.

"You're just being suspicious and paranoid again," he replied.

"Do you think I don't know what's going on between you and that whore?"

Jim heard Sandra's voice and realized she had returned. He hated to have her exposed to Brittany's outburst but there was no way of preventing it.

"Think what you want, Brittany," Jim said. "But please don't victimize the boys with your erratic behavior."

"Don't come home tonight."

With that final remark she left with Rodney and Kevin. Sandra later told Jim that on her way out Brittany stopped in front of her and called her a two-bit whore.

Jim did not go home that night and Brittany made futile attempts to have him come back and reason things out. She tried to make him go on a guilt trip by constantly reminding him of what their split was doing to the boys. Rodney was still bullying Kevin but now the younger boy was learning to defend himself. The burden of acting as a referee was too great. She definitely needed a man in the house and she could even forgive Jim's indiscretion. But Jim's mind was set on not returning. He moved in with Sandra and their blissful relationship made it too difficult for him to go back to the turmoil of his married life. Above all, Sandra could satisfy Jim sexually with no religious hang-ups. Brittany finally gave up and filed for a divorce. She told Jim she would move back to Cranston and take Rodney with her. Jim would have custody of Kevin.

"You and your Montana slut should thank me for not dumping the 'bad seed' on you," she told Jim. "But bear in mind, I am only doing it for Rodney. He is still my son and a problem child needs a qualified parent to raise him."

Brittany was able to get the house, which she already had put up for sale. All other assets were split in half according to Texas law. Jim had been promised that he would eventually become a full partner of Gulf Coast Ship Agencies and he was pleased that the Paradissis brothers had not as yet officially rendered that offer to him. It certainly would have complicated the community property settlement.

~ ~ ~

Jim and Sandra were married in a civil ceremony at the courthouse in Sweet Grass County, Montana. They took Kevin, now nine years old, and he seemed to particularly enjoy the wilderness and open spaces that Houston lacked. Sandra's parents threw a small get-together for them after the wedding and friends let them use their cabin by the Crazy Mountains north of Big Timber. Sandra explained that one theory why the mountains got their name was that an elderly Indian woman was isolated there by her kin because she had become too frail and senile to function in the community. Her isolation caused her to become insane.

"Maybe that's where Brittany should have been dumped," Jim said, knowing that Kevin could not hear him since he was busy fishing. Jim and Sandra had decided not to be too critical of Brittany since they knew Kevin still carried a lot of love and affection for his mother. He even called Brittany and Rodney in Rhode Island to let them know about the fish he caught. Jim took a photo of his son proudly displaying his prize so he could mail them to Rhode Island. Photos were also taken of the deer that occasionally came near the cabin.

During the return flight to Houston, Kevin stated this was the best time he ever had and that he even enjoyed it better than Disney World. It was also wonderful not to have Rodney around him.

The Paradissis brothers treated them with typical Greek generosity upon their return. They threw a lavish party in their honor and invited influential people in the maritime industry including oil brokers, ship owners' representatives, and charterers. The brothers, however, did not follow up on their promise to make Jim a partner and he did not bring it up. He was quite satisfied with the raises he and Sandra received. They were both determined to work doggedly to make the company grow.

Saad Hussein, the local representative of the Saudi Arabian Line, seemed to enjoy the party and was drinking excessively despite his Muslim faith.

"Those canapes, do they contain pork?" he asked Jim in his well pronounced BBC accent. Obviously, like many Saudis, he went to a finishing school in London. He was a well-built man of average height in his early forties and sported a thick moustache. Saad could have passed as Omar Sharif's brother.

"I'm not too sure," Jim replied.

"Maybe I should stay away from them. Pork is against my religion," Saad said, downing a Chivas on the rocks. Later on, he seemed to want to socialize with Jim and Sandra and expressed his gratitude for the fine agency work Jim was rendering to the Saudi government.

"My wife Leila and I would love to have you over for a Middle Eastern dinner," he said. "But no liquor. I don't imbibe at home because of my sons."

"I don't think we'll even miss it," Jim said.

Saad and Leila lived in an expensive rented apartment not too far from the posh Galleria shopping mall. Their furniture, which was bought in the Middle East, gave it an *Arabian Nights* aura. Leila was very good-natured. She seemed to be a liberated Arab woman, fashionably dressed and a heavy smoker. Their dinner was served by a Filipino maid and their twin sons ate separately so as not to distract the adults. Sandra commented that Jim's son Kevin was close to their age.

"You should have brought him along," said Leila. "Samir and Mohamed have not made too many American friends."

The food served was an exotic extravaganza: tabouli salad, babaganoush dip with toasted pita bread on the side, humuus, roast goat, pilaf rice, and baklava for dessert. A drink similar to Hawaiian Punch with pieces of fruit and almonds inside, which they called "sharbat," accompanied the meal.

To compensate for the lack of liquor, Saad offered everybody genuine Cuban cigars, in which they indulged with their Turkish coffee. Jim smiled as he watched Sandra trying to act sophisticated as she spoke and puffed.

"Is it common in Saudi Arabia for women to smoke cigars?" she asked Leila.

"Of course not," Leila laughed. "I do it because I enjoy it and Saad doesn't mind."

"She does many things here that she would not do back home," Saad said. "The most important thing, of course, is driving a car."

"I'd love to someday visit your country," Sandra said, trying to be polite.

"It isn't possible now," Saad said. "Our country will only allow you in if you are there on business or on a pilgrimage to Mecca. I hope this will some day change."

"That part of the world is so vital to us," Jim said. "The energy crisis has truly shown Americans that they are not as energy self-sufficient that they thought they were."

"Ah, yes," said Saad. "You can no longer tell us to go drink the stuff."

The conversation now centered around the volatile situation in the Middle East. The 1973 Arab-Israeli war had truly given the Arabs a new image and there were now talks about President Anwar Sadat visiting Israel. Jim thought Sadat was a good man. Saad agreed but mentioned that a lot of Arabs felt he was a traitor. In Saudi Arabia people thought that they were the true guardians of Islam because of Mecca. Thus it was only appropriate for the Saudi royal family to visit the holy Muslim sites in Jerusalem before Sadat.

Saad then asked Jim if he were interested in joining the local American-Arab society. It was a social club with no political attachments and consisted mostly of Arabs and American oil executives who had an interest in the Middle East.

CHAPTER FOUR

The Houston Chronicle
November 18, 1975
"New points"

Submitted by Jim Blackburn

> Rabbi Jack Segal's disgust over Egyptian President Sadat
> being gifted with a .45 revolver in Houston would be alle-
> viated if he would ponder on the following:
> Sadat is a man of peace. His courage in defying the
> hawks in the Arab world and his statements about Israel
> being a reality makes him eligible for a Nobel Peace Prize.
> I feel it is erroneous to search for symbolism in a gra-
> cious act of friendship and hospitality. The donor of the
> revolver might have been looking for a typical gift from
> Texas. However if the donor had symbolic intentions, the
> gun could have reflected a policy of fairness in U.S. military
> aid to the Middle East.

As a member of the American Arab Society, Jim attended the reception
given to President Sadat at the ranch of an oilman and witnessed his being
presented with the revolver. Sandra accompanied Jim and appeared dazed as
she shook hands with the president and Mrs. Sadat as well as Nancy
Kissinger. It was an extravagant affair since the oilman had purchased prize
Arabian horses during his trips to the Middle East and proudly displayed
them to his guests. There was also a theatrical presentation of the Texas fron-
tier days which made the bodyguards jumpy when the blank shots were fired.
    Although Saad and Leila had returned to Saudi Arabia, Jim remained
active in the American Arab Society. Sandra enjoyed the social get-togethers
but was concerned about Jim becoming too involved in the society since they

29

had Jewish friends and Jim and Sandra's photo appeared in the newspaper's society column whenever they attended one of the club's balls.

The Arabs had become unpopular after the killing of Jewish athletes at the Munich Olympics but this did not prevent Jim from being vocal in his support of their struggle. He became a board member of the American Arab Society. They would meet every week at the office of the American Arab Chamber of Commerce and in between the planning of the next social event, they discussed the ways and means to propagate the Arab cause.

The society's president was a Palestinian refugee called Ahmed Hilal.

"When I left my home town of Ramallah and had to endure the hardship of refugee life, I promised my dying father that I would always make it my goal to spread the word about our suffering," he told the board members.

Trevor Robins, the owner of Panther Oil Exploration Co., sat by his side and was always prepared to offer the society the financial support it needed. At one meeting it was unanimously voted to build an American Arab Cultural Center which would rival the Jewish Community Center. Trevor advised the board members that a number of his oil associates were willing to contribute to the purchase of the land.

"Houston's economy is based on oil and it is vital for us to make people realize that the Arabs play a big part in our prosperity," Trevor told the board members. He then referred to the recent suggestions by some city council members to put a ban on Saudi Arabian flagged–vessels in the Port of Houston until a permanent peace was established in the Middle East.

"This is total insanity," Trevor said. "The Zionist influence in American policy has to come to an end. Haven't we learned anything during the oil embargo? If we do not act to stop this insanity we can expect more line-ups at the gas stations this winter."

Jim volunteered to make out a petition addressed to the city council and port director and have it signed by several notable names in the maritime industry. This effort was successful since the Houston City Council voted against the boycott.

"I am very disappointed in you." Spiro Paradissis personally visited Jim at the office. "Your political views and associations are your own business but don't use your position with us to enhance your propaganda."

"I'm sorry you feel that way, Spiro," Jim replied. "I, too, am disappointed in you for not allowing me to express my views."

"Express your views all you want. But, Jim, everybody in the business knows who you work for. Sending out a petition to people we deal with makes our company involved in your cause. That's too risky. Especially when you have a ship in port loading vegetable oil for the Israeli government and they are asking you to send a rabbi to go down and kosherize the tanks before loading."

Spiro was trying to act stern but it seemed like his own remark triggered a jovial smile on his face.

"Come off it, " he said. "Stop being a defender of the underdog!"

The argument went on for a long time with Jim's spirit of contradiction at full force. Sandra did her best to break it by walking in Jim's office and offering Spiro coffee. Spiro accepted but continued with his reprimand of Jim.

"Maybe familiarity does breed contempt after all," Spiro said. "My brother and I have treated you like a relative and now you seem to forget that you owe us your respect."

"You have my respect," Jim said. "But not my heart and soul."

Spiro angrily walked out of the office.

"Was all that necessary?" Sandra asked. "For just once, Jim, why don't you try to be diplomatic and not say what's in your chest?"

"I've had it with those controlling Greeks. If I was to quit and start my own company, I bet a lot of their major clients would switch agencies."

As it turned out, Jim did not have a chance to quit. That same day he received an unexpected visit from the FBI. Jim had not seen Ron Fabri in over two years and assumed that the bureau had found another way to keep tabs on Soviet ships besides interrogating the agent.

"I understand you and your lovely wife are active members of the Arab Society." Ron Fabri said.

Jim's heart temporarily stopped beating. Surely, the government was not going to dictate to him what organization he was allowed to join? After all, he had fought in Vietnam supposedly to safeguard world freedom. Big brother did not exist in the U.S.

"Yes, Sandra and I attend their social functions," he said nervously. "I hope we're not breaking any laws."

Ron Fabri laughed.

"I saw your photo in the newspaper. You have a very lovely wife."

"Thank you. You probably noticed that she also works here."

"How can I fail to notice?"

Jim called Sandra to his office and introduced her to the FBI agent.

"Mr. Fabri is here to inquire about the Soviet vessels. Could you get me the *Komsomolets Kubani* file?" asked Jim, referring to the Soviet vessel that sailed from Houston two weeks ago. Sandra brought Jim the file and left the office.

"Okay, now you can ask me what you need to know."

"I did not come to see you about a Soviet ship," Ron Fabri said. "Tell me what you know about the *Mavrodaphne*."

"That's a molasses ship that belongs to my bosses. She makes frequent voyages to and from Buenaventura, Colombia."

It finally dawned on Jim why Ron Fabri came to visit him. Like many vessels arriving from Colombia, the *Mavrodaphne* was being scrutinized for any involvement in the drug trade. In fact, during her last arrival, U.S. Customs came onboard for a thorough search with drug-sniffing dogs. Joe, who was the agent onboard, said he felt a sense of relief when they were unable to find any illegal substance.

"What's her next ETA to the Port of Houston?" Ron Fabri asked.

"She should be at the Galveston Bar at 2000 hours tonight and dock at City Dock One East around 4 A.M."

"Does she always arrive late at night?"

"It's been that way recently."

Jim was getting aggravated by the cross-examination. He looked Ron Fabri straight in the eye, evoking a message of *What the fuck do you want of me?*

"You will, of course, advise the port authorities of any changes in her ETA," Ron, Fabri said.

"Don't I always?"

Before leaving, Ron Fabri told Jim he was a hard-working man and the FBI always appreciated his cooperating with them.

Jim sensed some trouble brewing and decided to personally meet the *Mavrodaphne* in the early hours of the morning. As expected, U.S. Customs was waiting, with dogs, for the ship to be tied up. In addition to Customs and Immigration, Jim noticed somebody from the U.S. Marshall's office holding a document in hand that looked familiar. The ship was about to be seized. Before the gangway was lowered, Jim went to a pay phone and called Spiro Paradissis. Notwithstanding the fact that Spiro would have his sleep disturbed, Jim felt that he should alert his boss that the ship might be in trouble. He was hoping that Spiro would tell him that the ship was being seized because of a large sum of money owed to some creditor and that the matter would be resolved during office hours. From past experience, Jim knew that this was the reason a ship was normally seized by the U.S. Marshall and not allowed to leave the port district until the matter was resolved.

Helen Paradissis answered the telephone. She sounded agitated and was speaking in between sobs.

"They raided our home and took him away," she said. "Both Spiro and Mario are in jail."

After going onboard, Jim found out that a bag containing close to five million dollars worth of Colombian cocaine was dumped by the *Mavrodaphne* on her way to the city docks. It landed on the roof of a warehouse and following a tip, the FBI arrested a man who was waiting to have it picked up. Spiro and Mario had been involved in the drug trade since they became the owners of the *Mavrodaphne*. This time they were caught.

CHAPTER FIVE

The year was 1980. Jim and Sandra had become millionaires. The collapse of Gulf Coast Shipping Agencies proved to be a blessing to them since Jim was able to start his own company and obtain a number of the Paradissis brothers' valuable accounts.

Jim and Sandra worked as a team and made yearly trips to London, Athens, Piraeus, Rotterdam, and Moscow to visit the people they dealt with and to recruit new clients. They always presented an image of hard work and honesty and their agency fees were lower than most of the competition. Sandra also found time to attend the University of Houston. After graduating in economics, she obtained licenses in freight forwarding and customs brokerage. Out of convenience, they started a separate company near the Houston International Airport so she could clear with Customs the spare parts consigned to the ships they handled.

Jim had no regrets about leaving Brittany. He had accepted the fact that Sandra was dead set about not having children and their interest in making their business grow contributed to their maintaining a very harmonious relationship.

Rodney, who attended Portsmouth Abbey in Rhode Island, stayed with them every summer for four weeks and the two brothers would then fly together to Cranston so Kevin could spend some time with his mother. Rodney and Kevin got along fine but it was obvious that Kevin had learned to tolerate his older brother since their stay together was not a permanent thing. The pep talk Jim would give his younger son prior to Rodney's arrival seemed to work.

Both Jim and Sandra were proud to see what a gentle and sharing person Kevin was turning out to be, unlike his brother, who seemed to have retained his childhood bullying and controlling traits. Brittany's determination to reform the "bad seed" apparently had failed. The one consolation was that Rodney's grades at Portsmouth Abbey were excellent. But he also became a know-it-all. At sixteen, he could discuss politics and current events in a rational and grown-up manner.

Kevin, who attended Kinkaid Academy in Houston, was an average student, very sports minded, and like most fourteen-year-olds, he was beginning to take an interest in the opposite sex. His popularity with girls seemed to trigger pangs of jealousy in his older brother.

Sandra became very close to Kevin but made no effort to break the ice with Rodney. Like Kevin, she tolerated him since his stay with them was always temporary.

During Rodney's visit, Jim received an unexpected telephone call from his mother in Providence, Rhode Island. It caught him by surprise, since Brittany had managed to alienate Jim and his parents after the divorce. She used religion as a weapon and kept reminding them that Jim and Sandra's marriage was not recognized by the Catholic Church. Jim tried to be courteous to his mother on the telephone and did not bring up the fact that they hadn't spoken to each other in over three years.

She was calling him about his twenty-five-year-old sister Martha. Martha apparently could not keep a job. She had dropped out of college, was still living at home, and was gallivanting at bars almost every night. She was rapidly spending the inheritance her father had left her when he passed away one year ago. Jim's mother was begging him to accept Martha and offer her a job in Houston.

"She needs an older man to guide her," she said. "You owe this to your father, Jim. Remember, you didn't even bother to attend his funeral mass and burial."

Feelings of guilt and shame possessed him. He and Sandra were on a business trip to Europe when his father died and because Brittany had caused a rift between him and his parents, he did not endeavor to return to the U.S. for the services. He knew he would have no problem persuading Sandra to accept Martha, but to show his mother that he respected his wife's decisions, he told her, "I'll have to discuss this with Sandra, Mom, since our business is jointly owned. We'll just have to call you back."

He spoke to Sandra and she had no objection to Martha working for them. In fact, she told Jim she was looking forward to meeting his younger sister. It was over ten years since Jim had seen her and he could not be too judgmental of her since he felt that his mother, who always babied her, was responsible for some of her character flaws.

That night before falling asleep, Jim had recollections of his youth. He remembered how his father worked hard as a CPA and adhered to the notion that as long as he was the sole breadwinner he had fulfilled his duty as a good parent. Not once did he attend any of Jim's school functions and never displayed any pride in the fact that Jim was an A student. Jim always felt that his mother was guilty of the sin of commission and his father the sin of omission.

Jim and his sons woke up in time for them to make their 8 A.M. flight. Since it was Saturday, Sandra decided to sleep in and not join them in the trip to the airport. Jim gave each of his sons $15 pocket money in case they got hungry during the two-hour stopover in Atlanta. Brittany was to meet them when they arrived in Providence and Martha was to accompany Kevin on his return trip.

"Good luck with Aunt Martha," Rodney told his brother. "I can't say I envy you."

"Why don't you let your brother decide for himself if he likes Martha or not?" Jim asked Rodney.

"My brother's a 'chooch' in matters of life and he needs to be cautioned about women like Martha," Rodney replied.

Jim had not heard the word "chooch" since he moved to Texas. "What the hell do you mean?"

Rodney answered his father in a deep voice, "Aunt Martha's a dyke."

Martha Blackburn came to Houston with Kevin a month later. Her hair was long and blond, and she stood like an Amazon. Her New England accent gave her an irrepressible charm. Jim had not mentioned his sister's sexual orientation to Sandra and was determined not to discuss it with Martha unless he brought it up herself. He had envisioned his sister as being very masculine and was a little concerned because of the homophobic mentality that dominated the maritime industry. But despite his upbringing by a neurotic mother, Martha acted as straight as any ordinary Jane.

Martha was to stay with Jim and Sandra and after a couple of months of training, she would be sent to Galveston to open a new branch office. The port of Galveston was becoming busy because of two grain elevators, a sulfur dock, and Todd Shipyards, where ships would dry-dock for repairs.

"The port of Texas City is only a fifteen-minute drive from Galveston and that is where a lot of the big name oil refineries can be found," Jim told Martha. "The two things that bug me about Texas City is the pollution and the lack of security at the port entrance. They experienced the most devastating refinery explosion in U.S. history and here they do nothing about protecting the port from terrorist activities. With the killing of athletes at the Munich Olympics, they should be aware of the dangerous times we're in."

Jim did not mention the fact that he was once active in the American Arab Society. This proved to be a passing phase. He got fed up with the infighting between the society's members. It seemed like the Saudis, Egyptians, and Palestinian members were power playing and competing against each other. The bloody civil war in Lebanon also contributed to the discord.

Contrary to his mother's negative description, Martha turned out to be a good learner and eager to work hard.

"How would you rate the port of Houston?" he asked.

"It's the third busiest port in the U.S. after the port of Southern Louisiana and New York. Not bad for a man-made canal that was built because Galveston was too hurricane prone."

Jim also explained that since Houston was not a deep-sea port, it could not accommodate the modern supertankers when they were too deep. These would partially discharge their cargo into smaller vessels outside of the sea buoy until they reached the required draft of 39'06.

"We call that a 'lightering' operation," Jim said. "It's a fast way of us making money since we charge agency fees for more than one ship."

Jim did not hesitate to divulge the different ways maritime companies raised their revenues. Although some of them sounded unorthodox, he explained to his sister that they were accepted tricks of the trade.

"We ask for port expenses before a ship arrives and wait at least three months before we honor most of the invoices for services rendered to the ship. That way the money we receive from the owners is accruing interest."

"Isn't this like money laundering?" Martha asked.

"There is no maritime dictionary of ethical practices. Especially when all agencies do the same thing."

Jim went on to explain the other techniques of fast money. Kickbacks were received from ship chandlers, ship repair services, tugboat assistance companies, and even divers when they were assigned to underwater surveys.

"It's a highly competitive industry. We are surrounded by warring vultures ready to pounce on a ship as soon as it docks."

Jim thought of the Paradissis brothers when he made this statement. He had never visited them at their prison cells in Huntsville, Texas, but had once called Helen Paradissis, who told him Spiro was proud of his accomplishments with his new company. At least he knew his former accounts were in good hands.

Two weeks after Martha's arrival, Jim was told that the owners of the MT *Eloiside* that was docked at Todd Shipyards had contaminated cargo tanks. They decided to have the vessel destroyed in order to generate some insurance payments since the ship could not be sold. The plan was to take the *Eloiside* to a deep-sea anchoring position and have her exploded. The ship would travel, laden with explosives, on a dead engine assisted by tugs. The owners wanted Jim to board another vessel and follow the *Eloiside* so he could witness the explosion and write a report for the insurance company. Jim thought this would be a good experience for Martha and he asked his sister to join him. Women were not the norm in the maritime industry and Jim knew he was taking a risk. The whole operation would last three days.

They boarded the Norwegian-flagged MT *Joy* to the anchoring position where the explosion was to take place. The waters were murky and choppy. Martha appeared a bit seasick but said she enjoyed the challenging nature of the trip. The excitement was heightened when they noticed sharks swimming alongside the ship.

36

It was a sad, stirring moment when the *Eloiside* exploded and sank. So sad that it brought tears to some of the crewmen, as if they were witnessing the execution of a loved one.

On the journey back, Martha revealed her homosexuality to Jim. They were alone on the upper deck. It had just turned dark and they were admiring the approaching lights of the city of Galveston. Martha said her homosexuality had bothered her to the point of attempted suicide but then she found others who accepted her with open arms and made her rid herself of the guilt feelings she bore. Martha did not blame her mother for her sexual preference. Her homosexuality was something she was born with. She would have been gay regardless of who her parents were. In fact, her overly straight demeanor was in rebellion to the way her mother had raised her.

Jim put his arm around his sister's shoulder and assured her that he and Sandra would never judge her by what she did in the bedroom.

"Thank you for making it easy for me to get it off my chest," Martha told Jim.

They returned home tired from their trip. Sandra advised Jim that while they were away, Joe, who Jim had retained as an agent after the other company folded, had a $10,000 cash advance to one of the ships in port stolen from his briefcase. Jim was perturbed not only because of the stolen money but also because if he reported it to the insurance company, Joe would never again be able to be bonded for delivering money to the ships. Jim had always trusted Joe and he knew that he would not have jeopardized his career for $10,000.

"I hate to say it," Jim said. "But we might have to absorb it."

This infuriated Sandra, who wanted to either report it to the insurance company or arrange a payment plan involving deductions from Joe's paychecks.

"He's married and has two kids," Jim said. "He can barely make it on his present salary."

"Maybe that'll teach him to be more careful with the ships' payrolls. Who ever thought of leaving a car unlocked in a waterfront neighborhood?"

The argument, in front of Martha, was lengthy and it ended with Sandra withdrawing to the bedroom and slamming the door.

"You have a heart of gold," Martha said to Jim.

"Since she started working at the airport she seems to have forgotten what an agent goes through and how difficult it is to hire the right people," Jim said.

The conversation then led to Martha asking Jim if his marriage was a happy one. Jim replied that he had no regrets about leaving Brittany but the second time around was far from being wine and roses. To a certain degree he and Sandra had learned how to give and take but many times there was no compromise. Sandra was a business whiz and had it not been for her talents, he doubted the company they formed could have succeeded. Sometimes, however, he wished she could be a little more humane in her interaction with others.

"She's going to win," he said. "We'll either have to get our money from the insurance company or from Joe."

Jim had found somebody to confide in. He now knew that he could always turn to Martha when he felt the need to open his heart to somebody. He was sorry that fate had separated them for so long. Martha was only six years old when Jim left home. He was sorry that he was not there when Martha went through puberty and discovered that she was a lesbian. The advice Jim would have given her could have prevented the inner turmoil she must have experienced.

But now Martha was in Texas. The Galveston office grew rapidly and sometimes Jim felt like calling his mother to thank her for sending him the "burden" she carried.

In 1984 Jim acquired the SOHIO tanker account, which would generate approximately twenty ships per month in Texas City. Thus he had to spend a lot of time in the Galveston office. He trusted Martha but because SOHIO was a special account, he felt that his intervention was necessary. SOHIO chartered vessels to pick up crude oil from Valdez, Alaska, then discharge the cargo at a pipeline in Chiriqui Grande, Panama. The cargo would then be loaded by another chartered vessel for discharge at the Arco or Amoco terminals in Texas City. Since the Alaska pipeline was built, this operation became the easiest means of Alaska crude reaching the U.S. Gulf Coast. The crude oil would then be refined into other chemicals at the Texas City refineries. The SOHIO account gave Blackburn Shipping Agency a lot of prestige and Jim was aware of the fact that the competition was waiting for one slip-up so they could offer their services to replace his company.

Galvestonians were generalized as being a very cliquish people. They were islanders and in many circles being a "BOI" (Born on Island) gave one an assumed sense of aristocracy. This mentality, however, did not deter Jim from making himself a name on the island. He made Martha join the local Optimist Club so she could get involved in civic matters as well as the Propeller Club of the United States that held monthly get-togethers.

Like he did in the *Houston Chronicle*, Jim now wrote to *The Galveston Daily News* to express his opinion on things of interest to the island. One letter, which was published on April 29, 1984, brought many flattering comments from businesses on Mechanic Street where the Blackburn Shipping Agency was located.

What's in a Name?

To Mr. George P. Mitchell, the name "Ship's Mechanic Row" must have an obsessive ring to it since he is once again using an encroaching tactic to make it replace the present "Mechanic Street."

Since the Galveston City Council voted against a full name change for the street in the past, Mr. Mitchell is now applying for another sectional change between 22nd and 23rd Streets. If passed, the cost to the city would only entail the changing of street signs. But to me the expense would be far greater since it would involve the reprinting of letterheads (including business cards, envelopes, and various commercial forms) and advising correspondents and directories of the name change.

"Ship's Mechanic Row" might evoke mental associations with times gone by, but in the maritime industry (where ships belong) the name is inaccurate and unappealing. The word "mechanic" does not exist in a maritime glossary of terms. There do exist ship's engineers, machinists, greasers, wipers, and even donkeymen, but no mechanics. Moreover, the word "row," according to Webster's Dictionary, is a "street or area dominated by a specific kind of enterprise or occupancy." Such is definitely not the case with Mechanic Street.

Galveston's gratitude to Mr. George P. Mitchell is beyond reproach, but I feel we have already expressed it by bestowing upon the area where his beloved Tremont House is located the name of "Ship's Mechanic Row."

George P. Mitchell, the billionaire oilman and developer, was seldom challenged. He was born on Galveston Island. The native son, who had made good and now lived in Houston, was revered for his investments in the city of his birth. Thanks to him, Galveston was going through an esthetic revival with the old hotel he restored and the new one he built facing the seawall. The new trolley cars that clanked past the historic Victorian homes were also his idea and the "Island King," as he was often called, even reintroduced the Mardi Gras parades à la New Orleans. Mitchell would proudly walk the Strand Street tourist area during the Mardi Gras or yearly Dickens festival, shaking the hands of those who recognized him as if he were running for a political office Even Jim shook his hand and introduced himself. Obviously Mr. Mitchell did not connect his name with the letter he wrote to *The Galveston Daily News* since he just said, "Pleased to know you, pardner," and walked away.

Jim stayed with Martha and her companion, Angela Garcia, when he came to Galveston. Society began to show some tolerance toward homosexuals and a lot of them were coming out of the closet. Sadly, this tolerance was short-lived when a new disease called Acquired Immune Deficiency Syndrome (or AIDS) began spreading among gays, Haitians, and hemophiliacs. Very little was known about the disease except that it was very contagious and deadly. Although most of the AIDS research was concentrated on male homosexuals and drug users, lesbian relationships were also at risk because of their sexual practices. Jim was relieved to see Martha in a monogamous relationship since being promiscuous made one more susceptible to contacting AIDS. Angela, a local Chicana, had recently lost her job as a manager of a five-star hotel. The Reagan administration did little to promote research for a cure, and the deaths were increasing worldwide at such a fast rate that the disease would soon reach pandemic proportions. Jim worried about his sons who, he was sure, were sexually active, and the latest word was that AIDS was now claiming the lives of heterosexuals.

Rodney, now twenty, was on a scholarship at Rice University in Houston. He was in his junior year and his ambition was to become an architect. He was making A's in most of the subjects he took. Kevin, eighteen, was a freshman at Houston's University of St. Thomas. Jim was renting an apartment for his sons and was pleased to know that they had outgrown their sibling rivalry and got along splendidly. Rodney even told Jim that Kevin was dating a foreign exchange student from Brazil called Celia who would sometimes spend the night at the apartment.

"More power to my little brother," Rodney said. "I always make sure I let him have some of my condoms whenever she visits."

"What about you?" Jim asked. "Any romance in your life?"

"Nah. Too busy hitting the books. I know of a couple of 'urinals' I can go to when I need to relieve myself."

Jim remembered his visits to Yolanda on Navigation Street. It appeared that Rodney was getting to be a chip off the old block. But AIDS was unheard of during the Yolanda days.

"Please be careful, son," he told Rodney. "I'm sure you've heard of AIDS."

"Don't worry about me, Dad. Save your sermons for Aunt Martha."

Jim tried to figure out why his son had turned out to be so homophobic. He wondered if it had something to do with his attending Portsmouth Abbey. He did not remember Brittany being anti-gay. He and his wife were children of Aquarius who believed in harmony and understanding. Maybe the pendulum was now taking a swing the other way. The hippies had become yuppies and the future yuppies were now becoming narrow-minded bigots.

The annual crawfish boil was an event given by the Propeller Club of the United States in Galveston. It was a popular get-together mainly made up of men in the maritime business. The crawfish boil was held in a large hall. The men would wear bibs around their necks to prevent their getting their shirts soiled as they sucked the spicy crawfish heads. Rodney and Angela had accompanied Jim to the event and while they were waiting in line for the food, they heard somebody say, "Since when does the Propeller Club allow dyke members?"

Jim turned around and saw Mark Vinson, who worked for a competitor. He was ready to confront him but Martha pulled him away.

"Just ignore him," Martha said. "What good would it do to make a scene?"

They sat down and drank one beer after another as they peeled and ate the crawfish. When the door prize ticket was drawn, Martha found out that she was the winner. She walked up to the stage to pick up her prize and Mark Vinson shouted out "Yeah Dyke." This prompted Jim to walk to Mark's table and punch him. Mark made an attempt to strike back but it did not take too long for other men to run and separate them. Both Jim and Mark were trying to free themselves from the hold of others so they could swing at each other.

"I wonder what SOHIO would do if they knew their agent was a dyke?" Mark blurted with blood dripping from his nose.

Jim did not answer but was still trying to break loose and attack Mark. Martha had now intervened and pleaded with Jim to return to his table. The other men told Mark to leave the hall.

"Fuck you all," Mark said as he staggered out of the hall. "You're all dyke lovers."

The president of the Propeller Club spoke on the microphone and apologized for the disturbance. He begged everybody to carry on and have a good time. Lively Cajun music then blared through giant speakers and contributed to the "coon-ass" atmosphere of the evening.

"I'm sorry I'm an embarrassment to you," Martha said.

"Don't ever say that, Martha," Jim told his sister. "The only one who should be embarrassed is that scumbag. You're ten times the person he'll ever be."

Jim and Martha then realized that because of the noise and commotion, they probably were not able to hear their Motorola radio-telephones. Since they did not have any ships in the Galveston or Houston area, this did not bother them too much. Martha stood up and used her Motorola to call her answering service. Because they were in an enclosed area, the connection was full of static. She was able to decipher, however, that they had an urgent message for her or Jim. Jim quickly left the table and headed toward a pay phone and called the answering service. He found out that they were trying to contact him or Martha for the past two hours.

The message was from Sandra. She was informing him that there had been an accident and that Kevin was flown by helicopter to St. Luke's Hospital in Houston. Jim first tried to call Sandra but there was no answer.

He then called directory assistance and asked for the telephone number of St. Luke's Hospital. He dialed the number with a trembling hand. Jim was agitated and it seemed like forever before they connected him to the emergency room. Then came the announcement that hit him like a stab in the heart: "We regret to say that the patient passed away forty minutes ago!"

CHAPTER SIX

The press had a field day sensationalizing the tragedy. They referred to it as the "Cain and Abel" killing and did not omit stating that it happened when the father, the owner of Blackburn Shipping Agency, was at a crawfish boil in Galveston.

Rodney was depicted as a young man, gifted with a superior intelligence, who had a lot going for him but, according to those who knew him, had an evil streak. They failed to emphasize the fact that it was self-defense and an accident.

The story that was told to Jim was that Kevin had found out that Rodney was trying to seduce his girlfriend Celia. The brothers got into a scuffle and Kevin hit his head on the wall. It was a fatal blow and he died from internal injuries shortly after he was flown to St. Luke's Hospital. Celia testified and explained the incident in detail to the police, who were satisfied with what they heard. Rodney was not going to be charged.

For Jim, it was indeed a "Cain and Abel" tragedy. He attended Kevin's funeral in a melancholic daze. Sandra, Martha, and Angela were seated next to him and Brittany was in a separate pew sobbing uncontrollably. At her insistence, Kevin lay in a closed casket and Jim knelt in front of it and crossed himself before leaving the church.

Before driving to the cemetery, Sandra wanted to offer her sympathy to Brittany. Jim refused to join her. He sat in his car with Martha and Angela and watched Sandra give Brittany a hug. Jim was surprised to see that Brittany did not push her away. After all, was Sandra not the Montana slut who broke up their marriage? It seemed like Brittany was too absorbed in grief to mind Sandra.

Rodney did not make an appearance at the church or the cemetery. Jim thought the guilt and sorrow must have prompted him to slay home alone with his shame.

After the casket descended to the ground, Brittany walked toward Jim with a bitter look coming out of her teary eyes.

"Always, remember," she said. "This happened when the boys were in your care and not mine."

"I'm sorry you haven't succeeded in reforming your bad seed," Jim replied.

"May God forgive you, Jim," Brittany said before entering the car of the friends she was staying with.

There was no wake for Kevin. Jim was not in the mood to see anybody. Martha and Angela were spending the night at his home and the three of them retreated to the patio after Sandra went to bed. They drank Glenfidich Scotch and Jim could not control the tears that journeyed to his chin. Martha put her arm around her brother's shoulder.

"You have to carry on," she said.

"It is possible to forgive Rodney," Jim said. "But will I ever forget?"

"For your own piece of mind, Jim, forgive and forget," Martha replied.

"It's going to be extremely hard. I should completely disown Rodney and try to forget he ever existed."

That turned out to be a difficult task. For the next few nights Jim had recurring dreams of his sons. In some dreams, they were sitting next to each other on a swing set as children and Jim was pushing. It was in the backyard of the Montrose house but Sandra, not Brittany, was watching in the background. In another dream, they were all fishing in Montana and comparing the sizes of their catch. Rodney seemed to be annoyed that Kevin caught the biggest fish.

Jim woke up every morning feeling extremely fatigued and would sometimes erupt in fits of crying. Sandra recognized that he was going through a clinical depression and begged him to get help. He ignored her and found solace in consuming large amounts of straight scotch. He would drink himself to sleep.

Not a word was spoken to Rodney since Kevin's death. Sandra told him that Rodney had contacted her. He was vacating the apartment and moving back to Rhode Island. Three months later, Jim received a letter from his son.

> Dearest beloved Dad,
>
> I'm not sure if you'll ever read this letter, but I'm writing it mostly as a desperate means of purging myself of the guilt demons that have possessed me.
>
> Dad, I know I have hurt you and Mom profusely. Oh, what I wouldn't give to go back in time and make this thing never happen! Alas, it did happen. I now know what Oscar Wilde meant when he wrote, "We all kill the ones we love."
>
> Dad, please believe me, I loved my little brother. Getting to know him better when we shared an apartment are memories I will cherish forever. It is said that when we think about the past, we always recall the pleasant memories

instead of the negative ones. Dad, I'm begging you to forgive me. I have a lifetime ahead of me and my future happiness depends on your forgiveness.

One of the prices I had to pay was not obtaining a
degree from Rice University. There was no way I would
have shown my face on campus again after what I did.

I am now enrolled at the University of Kingston. It is
older than Rice (built in 1892) but not as prestigious. I truly
hope to make you proud of me some day, if only you'd let me.

Please Dad, forgive me. I'll always love you.

Your son,
Rodney.

Jim tore the letter up and threw the little pieces in the living room fire-
place. He lit a match and watched the letter burn.

The shipping business was booming. Jim had fifteen employees in
Houston and five in Galveston. Sandra's airport office also grew and she had
four people in her employ. But Jim's mind was no longer in the business. He
would arrive late and leave early and his appearance had become almost
slovenly. It was quite a contrast to the tip-top dresser he used to be. When
he started the business, he established a dress code for his agents. They had
to wear a tie when they went onboard the ships, regardless of the Houston
heat. After all, captains were used to seeing their agents neatly dressed in
other world ports. T-shirts and blue jeans were definitely not allowed. Now
he had stopped setting the good example and the agents would show up casu-
ally dressed without being reprimanded.

At the line-handlers' Christmas party Jim got totally inebriated. It was
an open house affair that started 11 A.M. Around 5 P.M. he left, disregarding
an offer to be driven home.

He was on Navigation Street and decided to stop by Yolanda's place,
which he hadn't visited in over fifteen years. He knew the liquor he had consumed would probably impede his sexual performance but unless Yolanda
had changed, he was sure she would understand.

He was greeted by an overweight Chicana woman who he remembered
being called Maria.

"Yolanda died three years ago," she told him. "Too many drugs."

She offered somebody else who could satisfy him but Jim refused.

He proceeded home in a drunken state and shortly after he hit Interstate
10, he was stopped by the police. They made him get out of the car and take
a sobriety test. Having determined that he was unable to recite the alphabet
and walk in a straight line, they handcuffed him, pushed him in the police car,
and drove him to the station. There he was fingerprinted and had his photo

taken. They asked him if he was willing to take a breath test. Since this was the first time he ever got arrested for drunk driving, he thought the amount of alcohol he had consumed did not warrant any criminal arrest, and he consented to having the test done. The results indicated an alcohol content of .14, far greater than the accepted .10 limit. Jim was formally arrested and told he could not make a telephone call until the next morning when it was decided what the bond amount would be. He spent the night behind bars with four other inmates.

He could not get a wink of sleep since one black inmate was singing minstrel songs and the guards did nothing to make him stop. They were on an evening shift and sleep was not an issue. They were having fun listening to the old drunk's minstrel songs.

The next morning, Jim was told that the bail would be $1,000 He asked if he could use a telephone and made a collect call to Sandra. She showed up an hour later and Jim was released from jail. He retrieved his car and followed Sandra home.

"What the hell is wrong with you, Jim?" Sandra asked.

"I'm going through an inner hell, Sandra."

"If you won't seek psychiatric help, I suggest we separate for a while. I just can't live like this."

Jim put his arms around her and started crying.

"Please don't leave me, Sandra. Right now I need you desperately."

He consented to seeing Dr. Eileen D'Attilio, a noted psychiatrist. She quizzed him extensively and he finally told her he had a fixation about his deceased son. He couldn't get Kevin out of his mind. He was there every single second. He had regrets about separating the two brothers. Had there been no divorce, maybe the boys would probably have established a better relationship and the tragedy would never have happened.

"Do you really think that growing up in an unhappy marriage would have solved everything?" the psychiatrist asked.

"Rodney was a difficult child, but maybe by working together with Brittany I could have made him turn out differently."

"I really think your biggest problem is booze."

Dr. D'Attilio prescribed an anti-depressant called Prozac, which was new on the market and seemed to be working miracles. She told Jim he had to stop drinking completely, especially since he was going to be on medication.

"Your best bet would be to join Alcoholics Anonymous."

"I've heard about that cult," said Jim. "Only winos fresh out of the alleys join AA. You also have to be religious. My spirituality has diminished since Kevin died."

"My other suggestion," said Dr. D'Attilio, "is for you to isolate yourself in a clinic for thirty days. There you will see professional counselors who will lead you step by step to sobriety."

Dr. D'Attilio suggested an out-of-town clinic since being isolated was imperative. Jim had his driver's license revoked for thirty days because of his DWI so the psychiatrist thought it was an ideal time for him to admit himself in a clinic. She suggested the Beaumont Neurological Clinic, about 100 miles east of Houston.

When Jim joined the clinic a sense of loneliness invaded him, even though surroundings were noisy and lively. He attended every group therapy session with a faked interest but would seldom participate in the discussions. Detoxification was very difficult and for five consecutive nights he lay in bed shaking and unable to sleep a wink. At the cafeteria he also felt tremors while he carried his food tray to the table.

One counselor, Sam Ladin, expressed his concern about his being so withdrawn.

"Come out of your shell," he told Jim. "The others refer to you as 'Mr. Introvert.' Is that what you want?"

"I guess it's hard being 'Mr. Congeniality' when you haven't slept in five nights."

"Give it time. You have been drinking yourself to sleep for a while and now your body has to adjust to a different lifestyle."

There were other counselors besides Sam but he seemed the one who took the most interest in Jim. Quite often, he would encourage Jim to participate by giving him more attention than the others.

"You keep stammering when you say 'I'm an alcoholic' and I want you to repeat it until you get it right," Sam said sternly. "Is it that difficult for you to face the truth?"

Jim knew that he had difficulty admitting his addiction. The clinic followed the Alcoholics Anonymous twelve-step method to sobriety and one's addiction had to be proclaimed when addressing the class. He always paused before saying the word "alcoholic," then stammered as if he had difficulty in pronouncing it.

Eventually some friendships were made at a slow pace. After a week at the clinic, he was able to befriend some of the younger patients. Most of them were sent there by their parents because of drug addiction. Somehow he felt more at ease with patients in their teens or early twenties. He would play Scrabble or Monopoly with them and laugh with them when they poked fun at some of the patients with serious emotional problems. One woman in her late sixties with a Phyllis Diller hairdo they labeled the "Space Cadet" because of the way she walked the hallway in a complete daze and mumbled to herself.

"She's holding Pluto," they would say or, "Fill'er up with oxygen so she can float."

However, Sam Ladin caught them doing it and confronted them about it at one of the counseling sessions.

47

"The healing process requires a lot of maturity on your part," he told the class. "Laughing at others not only shows childishness but also insecurity since that's what it takes to make you feel better about yourselves."

He then told Jim he could not believe he would participate in such a cruel and immature way of having fun.

At another session, Sam Ladin asked the class to think of the most appropriate color for temptation.

"Anger is red, jealousy is green, cowardice is yellow but temptation, an emotion most of us face every day, has no color."

"How about fluorescent purple?" one patient asked and the class laughed.

"Good choice," said Sam. "Flashing fluorescent purple."

He then asked the class to relate some of their struggles with temptation. Although he was Jewish he said that the "The Lord's Prayer" was the best spiritual expression that existed since people of all faiths could relate to it.

"Since we even ask God not to lead us into temptation, how can anybody deny the strength of that emotion?"

"Asking God not to lead us into temptation is inane," Jim said. "How can God, the kind, the compassionate, lead anybody into temptation? Is he an eccentric God who enjoys playing with our minds? I thought temptation was the work of the devil."

"God made the devil," said Sam.

Jim stood up. "Wrong, Sam, wrong! God made angels who later rebelled and became devils."

That was the first time Jim spoke up with enthusiasm. He remembered a letter he once wrote to the *Houston Post*.

> Mr. Billy Graham's using our earthly inferno as an omen of the second coming of Christ is a perfect example of a "witch doctor" type of piety. Let me remind Mr. Graham that Bobby Kennedy's assassin was exposed to the unreasoning beliefs which he advocates and they did not promote his salvation.
>
> What sort of a Messiah would permit violence, wary, and unrest before his arrival? If this is the Messiah Mr. Graham is referring to, I don't wish to meet Him when he gets here.

But now he was verbally expounding his convictions to a class. He went on to tell them that his God was different to theirs. In fact, he preferred to refer to it as a Higher Power instead of a God. His Higher Power was his friend and guide. He could laugh with him and try to console him when he was sad. Above all, his Higher Power did not punish people by bringing wars, hurricanes, and AIDS. He believed in evil and that life was a constant struggle between good and bad. He also believed that all prophets were divine since their link to the Higher Power was closer than his would ever be. Mankind's spiritual evolution was to expand until some day man would be able to better interpret the Higher Power that is engrained in him and spiritual unity would become a reality.

"You claim you're a Catholic but you sound more like a Baha'i. Have you ever thought of joining this faith?" Sam asked.

"I'm a Catholic only when I feel the need to worship since this is the only way I know how," Jim replied. "But I can't see myself being involved in organized religion."

"How about this notion of God creating angels and not devils? Do you believe in that?"

"Definitely not. I said it for the sake of argument."

"I think Jim Blackburn deserves a hand for finally coming out of his shell," Sam Ladin said and the class applauded.

"And how do you fight temptation, Jim?" Sam then asked him.

"I don't fight it, I suffer it."

At the next group therapy session Jim told the class about the tragedy that recently befell him and how it was so difficult to erase it from his mind. Although he had banished his son Rodney, there were times when he wished he could hold him in his arms and tell him he forgave him. But he was convinced that Rodney was 100 percent evil and forgiving an evil person would not make him change his ways. One patient suggested praying for Rodney but prayer, to Jim, was not an option. Rodney was too evil to be prayed for. He could never get rid of his demons.

After the second week at the clinic Sam asked Jim to see him for a private one on one. That meeting applied to all patients who had completed two weeks of sobriety.

"You still have another two weeks to go in this clinic," he told Jim. "After we release you, you still have to come here twice weekly to attend more group counseling sessions. You will be tested every time for drugs and alcohol. This will go on for another thirty days."

"I am a business owner," Jim replied. "I don't think I'll have time to drive here all the way from Houston."

"We can easily arrange for you to attend sobriety classes at a Houston clinic." Sam then reminded him that his DWI trial was going to be held in six months and his proving his total sobriety would affect the judge's decision.

Before leaving Sam's office, Jim asked him for a favor. "I wish to call my office," he said.

"It's against our rules. Complete isolation from the outside world is our number one requirement. But I will make an exception and let you use my phone on one condition."

"And what is that?"

"Get that fucking chip off your shoulder!" Sam barked.

Jim called Sandra and found out the company was being sued by a crewmember of the *Athenian Glory*, a tanker that discharged crude at Texas City four months ago. She told Jim to call Martha in Galveston to get the details. When he called Martha he found out that when the *Athenian Glory* was in port, a crewmember who had diabetes was taken to see Dr. Petrides. Since that doctor spoke Greek fluently, the transportation service was instructed to always take Greek crewmembers who needed medical treatment to see him. Dr. Petrides was retired from St. Mary's Hospital and examined his patients at his home. He prescribed the proper medication to the seaman and wrote him a diagnosis stating that he was healthy enough to go back to work onboard the ship.

When the ship was at sea, the crewmember developed gangrene in his right leg and it had to be amputated.

"So what had that got to do with us?" Jim asked.

"They are saying we chose the wrong doctor to examine the guy."

"Why don't they sue the doctor?"

"They are. Dr. Petrides is being sued, so is the transportation company which took the man to his home. St. Mary's Hospital is washing its hands from the whole affair since Dr. Petrides is no longer a part of their staff. This might cost our insurance company a bundle."

"Did you know Dr. Petrides was retired?"

"The only thing I was told was to send the seamen to his home instead of his clinic at St. Mary's."

Jim felt a sense of despair and at that moment he wished he had a glass of Chivas on the rocks in front of him. Thank God the treatment did not prevent him from lighting a cigarette. Sam Ladin watched him get agitated and when he finished his telephone call he surprised Jim by walking toward him and kissing him on the lips. Jim was stunned. He stared at him and had trouble finding the right words to say.

"Now you know," said Sam.

Still silently staring at him, Jim walked out of Sam Ladin's office.

At the next class they both acted as though they had agreed not to mention the incident. But the way Sam spoke to the class made Jim think he was dropping him hints about his sexuality. Sam explained that he was molested by his rabbi at the age of eleven. It was a traumatic experience but he kept it to himself since he feared his parents, who thought highly of the rabbi, would never believe him.

"I'm sure my childhood would not have been as emotionally tortured had I spoken to somebody about it," Sam told the class.

He then said that even though he was happily married and the father of three, his life was still challenged by sexual hang-ups.

"So you see, class, I'm just a feeble human being, flesh and bones, just like you."

Sam Ladin did not elaborate on what his sexual hang-ups were. When it came time for Jim to leave the clinic, he shook his hand and thanked him for being so understanding.

Jim was determined to start a new leaf when he returned home. He would take Sandra out for dinner almost every night and to prove his sobriety to her he always ordered Perrier to accompany his meal even though she ordered wine. It seemed like their married life had once again found the bliss and harmony that existed before Kevin's death.

Within a week, however, Jim found out something that would greatly affect his relationship with Sandra. He was checking the mail and noticed an envelope addressed to her that had a clinic's name on the letterhead. Thinking that Sandra was getting treatment at the clinic for an ailment she preferred not to discuss with him, he opened the envelope. It shocked him when he saw an invoice for an abortion performed on his wife.

"No wonder you were so anxious to get me out of the way," he told her angrily.

She nonchalantly explained to him that they had agreed not to have children. She kept her abortion a secret because she did not want to upset him.

"I lost a son, you insensitive bitch." He had never spoken to Sandra that way in the past. "Did you ever stop to think that another child would have alleviated the inner turmoil I went through?"

"Jim, I don't want any children. End of story."

CHAPTER SEVEN

On March 24, 1989, the *Exxon Valdez* grounded near Prince William Sound, Alaska, spilling 10,080,000 gallons of crude oil. It was not only an ecological disaster of dynamic proportions but also a grim day in the maritime industry. The United States Coast Guard created strong pollution regulations pertaining to vessels sailing in U.S. waters and the word was that in the next four or five years, all ships would have to be double-hulled. Moreover, since the captain of the *Exxon Valdez* was reportedly drunk, a new Coast Guard regulation prohibited the consumption of liquor onboard a vessel, regardless of its flag, that docked at a U.S. port.

Since Jim's business was primarily a tanker agency, he was experiencing tremendous losses. The SOHIO ships were no longer coming to Texas City and with the closing of Todd Shipyards and the Union Equity grain elevator, he was compelled to shut down the Galveston office and have Martha transferred to Houston. To save on rent, he also shut down the airport office. Sandra would share the main office to conduct the customs brokerage business.

Things did not improve in the next two years, mostly because of radical political changes in the world. The Soviet Union officially broke up on December 26, 1991, and the new Russia was having problems adjusting to a democratic system. A strict austerity program was introduced there. Russian ships trading in the U.S. had become very scarce.

Jim's company, which at one time had handled approximately sixty ships per month, had been No. 1 in the Houston/Galveston area for many years since it first opened. Now with only seventeen ships per month, Blackburn Shipping Agency had slipped to No. 5. His main competitors, such as Moran Gulf Shipping Agencies and Biehl and Co., surpassed him in the monthly volume of ships they handled.

In August 1990 Iraq invaded Kuwait and in January 1991 the United States led a coalition of nations to war against Sadam Hussein. Operation Desert Storm lasted four weeks. Kuwait was liberated after the Iraqi dictator ordered the burning of that kingdom's oil wells, causing a spillage of

130,000,000 gallons. A scarcity of oil was foreseen since the United Nations banned all trade with Iraq, the second biggest oil exporter in the world. This scarcity signaled better days in shipping but recovery was very slow.

Jim turned fifty-one in the summer of 1992. He had become prematurely gray and a middle-age paunch was becoming visible. He was not one to diet and exercise, so he wore a girdle out of modesty. Nevertheless, his health was excellent. He also remained sober since he left the clinic seven years ago and although he was reluctant to join at first, he faithfully attended the AA weekly meetings.

Sometimes he thought of Rodney but would make himself quickly erase that thought lest it would persuade him to sway toward forgiveness. He was still on Prozac and that greatly eased his tortured mind.

Jim's relationship with Sandra had turned sour since he found out about the abortion. He could not believe that the wife he once adored could turn out to be so deceitful. Since that day, Sandra and Jim remained compatible professionally but a curtain was drawn between them in their married life. They still had sex but not as often as they used to and she made sure he used a condom. She bluntly told him if she got pregnant, the baby would once again be aborted. That was her body and what she did with it was solely her business. Sandra, the innocent girl from Montana, turned out to be a bitch goddess.

Martha, too, was having her share of problems when she found out that her partner for life Angela was diagnosed with AIDS. She told Jim that although Angela had been unfaithful and promiscuous, she was still in love with her and could not see herself leaving her at a time when she needed her the most. It truly saddened her to see Angela suffer. She took a lot of time off from work to be with her at the hospital.

Jim followed the slogan of "One Day at a Time" in adherence to what he learned at the AA meetings. He wished, however, that the days would go by faster since things were bound to get better in the future. It definitely could not get worse than the present situation.

He finally sensed a glimmer of hope when he received a telephone call toward the end of 1992. The man spoke with a European accent that was difficult to pinpoint. He introduced himself as one Reginald Grech and he was calling from the island of Malta.

"My name is spelled G-R-E-C-H," he told Jim, speaking slowly as if enabling him to write it down. He said he received some very favorable comments about Blackburn Shipping Agency and wished to meet with him about agency representation. Mr. Grech told him he would be in London in a couple of weeks and would gladly pay for the flight expenses if he would meet him there to discuss his offer. What Mr. Grech had in mind was employing two of his ships for lightering operations in the U.S. Gulf.

"I understand the maximum draft in the Houston ship channel is still 39'06" brackish water," he told Jim.

Jim confirmed that this was correct.

"Do you know of any other company in your area that is involved in lightering deep tanker vessels?"

Jim felt that Mr. Grech was just testing him since everybody in the maritime industry knew that there were only two companies in the Houston/Galveston area that were involved in the ship lightering operation. Because most supertankers were now being built to load a greater volume of liquid cargo than previously, they were usually too deep to enter the Houston area. Some of the cargo had to be discharged to other vessels.

"There are only two companies in the lightering trade," he told Mr. Grech. "Skaugen Shipping and OMI Petrolink."

"That's what I thought. Now there will soon be three. Who knows, we might even put the other two out of commission."

Sandra insisted on going to London with Jim even if it meant her paying her own way. In London, however, Sandra preferred to go shopping at Harrods than join Jim when he went to meet Mr. Grech at the London Hilton. She promised not to overspend. Her main objective was to get a Harrods shopping bag to say she had been there.

Reginald Grech was in Jim's age bracket. He was tall, bald, and blinked his eyes when he spoke indicating a mild case of Tourette Syndrome.

"You seem to have a reputation in the business as being an aggressive go-getter," Reginald told Jim as they dined on Yorkshire pudding.

"Well, sir, I try to be," Jim replied.

"The word 'sir' does not exist in my vocabulary. I try to be as informal as Americans. Now when somebody mispronounces my last name, it's a different story." Jim realized that he had been guilty of that since he had pronounced Grech with a "ch" sound instead of "ck."

"*Grech* sounds too much like *wretch* and you'll find out I'm not too wretched once you do business with me," Reginald said jovially.

They discussed the agency fee for over one hour. Reginald was downing martinis while Jim stuck to Perrier with a twist of lime. They finally agreed to a $2,000 fee per ship. This fee would be all inclusive and except for long-distance telephone expenses and postage, there would be no added charges such as auto hire, agent's overtime, and husbandry expenses that were normally charged by most agents in the business.

"You will be assigned an average of two ships per week, taking into consideration the frequent fog and channel closure that you get in Houston. Weather permitting you'll be seeing three ships in one week. American shipping is going down the drain, which is good for us European ship owners."

It was a done deal. Before separating, Reginald Grech told Jim he was returning to Malta on Thursday and invited him to travel there with him and be his guest for the weekend. They would sign the contract over there.

"Since your wife is here with you and I am told you work as a team, she too is welcome to come to our enchanted island. The tickets are on me. You will find Malta to be very interesting. We are now becoming noticeable in the shipping world because we are following the path of Liberia and Panama and offering our flag to big-name ship owners."

Jim thanked him but when he returned to their bed and breakfast Sandra was not too enthusiastic about joining him to Malta. She felt that she would contribute more to the business if she stayed in London and tried to recruit new accounts by personally visiting them.

Malta was truly an enchanted island. The Grechs lived in a beautiful villa in the suburb of Madleina. It overlooked an awesome view of the Mediterranean that easily rivaled the French Riviera.

Melita Grech was charming and a doting mother to their sons Christopher, twenty-two, and Salvatoro, nineteen, and daughter Rachel, twelve. Reginald told Jim that although the boys lived at home, they had their own apartment to entertain women.

"We got that concept from the French who call it a *garconiere*. After all, men are men and why rush them into getting married? They should have their fun first."

Jim felt like telling him about the sad experience he had with his own two sons but kept quiet since it would reveal his failure as a parent. These two brothers were obviously taught at a young age to love one another.

The boys seemed to be fascinated by Jim's accent.

"They filmed the movie *Popeye the Sailor* with Robin Williams here and it was a real delight to see our island invaded by so many Americans," Reginald said. "We are, of course, used to the British since they colonized us for a number of years. For a while we had that bastard Mintoff as a leader and he encouraged Libyans to invest their money here. In fact, rumor has it that Khadaffi himself had found refuge in Malta when Reagan ordered his attack on Libya. Thank God Mintoff is gone and our new president is more pro-western."

"We, too, had elections last month and thank God, Bill Clinton will take office in January. I'm sure he'll be better than Bush, especially when it comes to the economy," Jim said.

"And here Bush was treated like a hero after Desert Storm. I suppose war victories mean nothing when the stomach is growling."

Before leaving Malta, Reginald took Jim to see the two tankers that would be involved in the lightering operation—the *Maj* and the *Melita*. On Sunday, he invited Jim to join him and his family on their yacht for a trip to the island of Gozo. There they had a seafood dinner, then walked the narrow cobblestone streets of the island. Reginald explained that some of the old homes were built in medieval times by the Knights of Malta. There were never changes made to the stone houses and inside the floors consisted of the same cobblestone and dirt found in the streets.

"In Houston, a home which is merely 120 years old is turned into a historical attraction," Jim said.

"I hope you'll spread the word about our island when you return to America. It's a pity most Americans cannot locate Malta on the map. And here we were the most bombed island during the Second World War."

"A lot of Americans can't find Texas on the map, much less Malta," Jim said.

When it came time for him to leave Malta, the whole Grech family saw him off at Lucca airport.

As soon as he arrived in London, Jim tried to call Sandra from the Gatwick airport. She was unavailable. He took a taxi to the bed and breakfast and there asked Mrs. Sims, the elderly lady who owned the place, if she knew where his wife was. She told him Sandra had mentioned going to the theater.

"She's very flighty, that one," Mrs. Sims said.

Sandra showed up around 11:30 P.M. And Jim could tell she had been drinking.

"I was invited to see ABBA at the Palladium by a Danish representative of the Maersk Line," she said. "I called on him this morning trying to recruit the account and he asked me join him. We had a couple of warm draft beers at a pub after the show."

Jim was not surprised that Sandra was revealing to him that she was out with another man. Their marriage had reached a stage where they could both do as they pleased. He had a feeling, however, that she had more than two beers.

"Were you at least able to obtain that account?" Jim asked.

"Not really. As you know Maersk has an office in Houston and their ships are boarded by Danish trainees learning the business. But Lars said he would pass the good word about us to the Houston office because sometimes they get very busy and need a subagent."

Sandra then went on to say she also visited Vitol Chartering, British Petroleum, and Shell International. The all looked like promising accounts, especially Shell International, who were very displeased with the services rendered by Moran Gulf Shipping Agencies.

"So you see, Jim, I was being productive while you were absorbing the Malta sunshine."

She asked him how he enjoyed Malta and he gave her all the details. He also showed her the contract he signed with Reginald Grech. Sandra was his business partner and he got her involved in everything pertaining to their company.

"You really should halve asked for more money," she said.

"These are hard times, Sandra, and beggars can't be choosy."

Sandra then told him not to get agitated because she was going to tell him something he might not like to hear.

"I am forty-three years old," she said. "I'm not getting any younger and I feel I haven't quite accomplished all my aims in life."

She then went on to tell him that she had investigated the possibility of studying international trade in London. She had visited several institutions, including the London School of Economics, and felt that a British education in international trade would surpass anything that was available in the United States.

"Britannia might not rule the waves anymore," she said. "But in the study of international commerce the Brits are still tops."

Jim told her he thought she had completely lost her mind but felt they should discuss it when they returned home in order to avoid making a scene in a small bed and breakfast.

The British Airways flight to Houston took eight hours. Sandra and Jim barely spoke to each other although Sandra put her head on his shoulder when she fell asleep. Jim did not know whether it was intentional or not and he himself was unable to fall asleep. He was angry and he was thinking of the words he would tell Sandra when they got home.

At home the argument they had was even bigger than the one when Sandra advised him of her abortion. He called her an ungrateful bitch who was set to destroy everything they had built together. She told him they were mismatched from the very beginning.

"You just wanted someone who was better in bed than Brittany and I was trying to find a way out of my relationship with Mark," Sandra told Jim.

Jim slept in the guest bedroom that evening.

The next morning Sandra begged him not to lose his temper and try to discuss the matter in a calm and civilized manner.

"I will only be away for three years," she said.

"How about the customs brokerage business?" Jim asked.

She told him Amber, her assistant, was quite capable of filling her shoes while she away. Furthermore, if Amber had any questions, she could easily answer them on the e-mail without accumulating exorbitant long-distance telephone charges.

Sandra and Jim went to work together. As soon as he walked in, Jim asked Martha to see him in his office to discuss the ships they presently had in port. When Martha shut the door and sat down, Jim told her about Sandra wanting to study in London.

"She's an ungrateful bitch," Jim said. "I guess we'll just have to make do without her."

57

CHAPTER EIGHT

The Houston Chronicle
June 7, 1994
"Viewpoints"

Submitted by Jim Blackburn:

> So Anna Vassillian, a French-born U.S. citizen, resents the fact that a draft dodger presided over D-Day's fiftieth anniversary celebrations ("Viewpoints," June 5).
>
> I wonder what her feelings are toward her former countrymen retreating from French Indochina and leaving the dirty laundry to the Americans?
>
> Unlike World War II, the Vietnam War did not involve a crazed demagogue who was trying to rule the world. Vietnam was a messy civil war and both Vassillian's native country and her adopted country tasted humiliating defeats after countless lost lives.
>
> President Clinton was born after D-Day so it is unfair to assume that he would have shied away from this valorous liberation. As for his dodging the Vietnam draft, Clinton was conscientious, patriot, and right.

Although Jim was in his fifties, he still adamantly held the belief he had as a young man that the war in Vietnam was a tragic mistake that should never have happened. He had read somewhere that even Jane Fonda was now being apologetic for her stance during that war, but not him. He had visited the Vietnam Memorial in Washington and found the names of some of the friends he lost. Some of them he did not even know had died in that dreaded combat.

Jim supported Bill Clinton. He thought he and his wife Hillary were two very intelligent people who were good for the country. When he heard somebody criticize the president for his sexual escapades, he'd say, "That's my kind of president!"

He was having his own sexual escapades since Sandra left for London. He went back to drinking and would frequent strip joints. A club called Caligula, where he got to know all the strippers by their first names, became his favorite haunt. Some of the strippers he would take home after the show for a night of sex. It was back to the Yolanda days but these women had more class than the Navigation Street whore and they charged a lot more.

Sandra kept her word about retaining her role in the customs brokerage business. She would often send e-mails to inquire about the company and returned to Houston whenever she had a break from her London studies. In Houston she was back to being Jim's wife. She never told him she missed him but the sex she had with him was performed with more passion than before she left. She would talk a lot about the courses she was taking and how her knowledge would benefit the company in the long run. Once she graduated and returned to the U.S., her aim was to obtain oil broker and ship chartering licenses. Although there was no more energy crisis, oil was still a commodity that played a vital role in the world's economy.

"When we think of oil we think about the gas we put in our tanks or the fuel we need to heat our homes," Sandra said. "Most people don't realize that we use oil in so many of the products in our every-day lives from aspirins to mouthwash."

She did not fail to remind Jim that her going to London was a good decision. The most important benefit was that she was able to recruit Shell International and other major accounts for Blackburn Shipping Agencies. There was no way Jim could now tell her that she had made a mistake. Sandra still had a year to go in London but was already making plans to move to a bigger home upon her return.

Jim's business was once again booming with the accounts Sandra brought and the Maltese lightering vessels that showed up on an average of three times per week. Reginald Grech had obtained the Exxon contract and had to add another ship, the *Saint Paul*, to his fleet. Jim also acquired the agency for the Norske Cruise Line and was not only able to reopen the Galveston office but also start an office in New Orleans. Martha, however, refused to go back to Galveston since Angela's health was deteriorating and she needed to be close to her lover.

One evening after he drove Sandra to the airport for her flight to London, Jim asked Martha to stay with him. When he arrived at Jim's home, Martha received a telephone call on her cellular phone from Memorial Baptist Hospital. They advised her that Angela had taken a turn for the worse. Jim tried to console Martha as she buried her face on his shoulder and wept. At the hospital they saw Angela with her eyes transfixed on the ceiling and breathing heavily. She had lost her hair and become skeletal. She seemed to recognize Martha and raised her arm when she approached her bed. Angela died in Martha's arms.

For the next few days, Jim shared his sister's moment of sorrow. Martha would constantly talk about Angela and Jim became a tolerant and patient listener. Eventually, he tried to divert Martha from her grief by going to a restaurant or a movie with her. One night they decided to go on the town and hit the favorite places they each frequented.

At Caligula, Jim paid Sharlee, one of the strippers, to do a table dance for them. She performed as though she was doing it just for Martha. She flaunted her breasts at her face. Martha fondly caressed her buttocks. Before they left Caligula, she made Martha write her telephone number on a napkin.

"The merry widow is not quite ready!"

They both laughed on the way home since they had discovered that there was hardly any difference between them when it came to the mating game. Because of a thick fog, the Houston ship channel was closed to traffic. This situation was dreaded by maritime agents since the Houston pilots would never advise them when the fog lifted and their assigned ships were boarded. Despite their annual salary of $200,000, the pilots acted as if they owned the port and would never cooperate with the agents. There was only one pilot association so the agent had no say-so in how they operated. Sometimes the agent would be up all night checking with the line-handlers to see if the fog had lifted and if the ship was boarded by the pilot.

Martha had a ship called the MT *Vanessa III* that had arrived at the anchoring position and waiting for the fog to lift. Since the ship was coming from Mexico, it was imperative for her to know her ETA at the dock so she could order the government officials accordingly. She called the line-handlers every hour and around 3 A.M. Jim told his sister to get some sleep. He would call the line-handlers himself. The ship was finally boarded at 5 A.M. and was scheduled to dock at her berth in Deer Park, Texas, around 9 A.M. Around 8 A.M. when Jim and Martha were on the way to the office, Martha received a call on her cellular phone from the line-handlers advising her that the berth assigned to the *Vanessa III* was occupied by another ship, the MT *Stolt Victory*. The terminal foreman had failed to advise her that the *Stolt Victory* was delayed in her cargo discharge operation and the Houston pilots did not bother to check the berth availability before boarding the *Vanessa III*. Since the *Stolt Victory* was now not scheduled to depart the berth until early P.M., Martha had to find a temporary berth for the *Vanessa III*. The expenses to the owners of the *Vanessa III* would be enormous and Martha sent protests by fax to both the terminal foreman and the Houston pilots, holding them responsible for all delays and expenses to the vessel.

"I doubt your protests will do any good," Jim said. "But it's good that you covered your ass."

Since he was sure the captain of they *Vanessa III* would probably be very upset over that incident, Jim decided to go onboard the ship with Martha. He usually responded to screaming captains with more tact and patience than his younger sister.

They went onboard the *Vanessa III* and were surprised to see the Norwegian captain very calm and collective.

"As you say in America, shit happens," Captain Bruland said as he poured some schnapps for them. He was a well-built Scandinavian in his early forties with a red beard and pitted face. His years at sea had given his face a salt water sort of roughness.

"*Schol!*" he said as he raised his glass. "We do not find any joy in complaining when things do not go our way."

Jim and Martha thanked him for being so understanding. A few minutes later, they heard a gong indicating that it was lunch time.

"We'd better get out of your way," Jim said.

"Oh no, please stay for lunch," Captain Bruland replied.

They discussed the cargo operation as they ate. The menu was typical Scandinavian: lobster soup, broiled halibut, steamed vegetables, an assortment of soft cheeses wrapped in silver triangle, and fresh fruit. Jim thought they must have a terrific baker onboard since the crusty bread was heavenly.

Just before they finished eating, Captain Bruland asked Jim if Blackburn was a common name in the United States. Jim advised him that there was a page full of Blackburns in the Houston telephone directory and the name was even more common on the East Coast.

"My ship's owner, Ingmar Pedersen, recently became engaged to a lady called Blackburn but I think she is English because they met in London. He has escorted her to many society balls in Oslo."

"Do you know her first name?" Martha, always the one for details, asked.

"I am not too sure," the captain replied. "It's either Sally or Sandra. She's a divorced woman in her forties."

Jim became agitated but not for too long. He quickly told himself the captain must be talking about somebody else called Blackburn. How could Sandra be engaged to a Norwegian ship owner when she was still married to him? It just didn't make sense. However, when they returned to Captain Bruland's office, he showed them a newsletter published by his company.

"Here, this is Sandra Blackburn with Mr. Pedersen," he said, pointing to a photo with Norwegian captions underneath it.

It was definitely his wife, Sandra. Jim even recognized the evening dress she was wearing. He remembered her having it altered just before they left for London since she had gained a couple of waistline inches. There she was with a broad smile on her face and a glass of champagne in her hand. A handsome Scandinavian-looking man dressed in a tuxedo was by her side, also smiling.

"They make a handsome couple," Captain Bruland said. "We all wish him good luck since his first wife died in a plane crash two years ago."

When they were in the car, Jim asked Martha to drive because he was too upset to think properly.

"That bitch," he kept saying. "That fucking bitch."

He decided not to stay at the office but took his own car and drove himself home. Once at home he had one drink of scotch after another and smashed a glass on the wall out of sheer despair. He couldn't help but think about his first marriage and kept asking himself if leaving Brittany was a good decision. True, the woman had her quirks but never had she cheated or lied to him. With Brittany, it was just a matter of tolerating her neurosis, and once in a while, visit Yolanda to sexually obtain what his wife could not give him. With Sandra, the sex was good. She did the oral sex thing every so often, and her business savvy helped him become rich. But what sort of a lying, cheating Jezebel had he married? And what sort of a stupid moron was he for not seeing through her?

He decided to call her around 9 P.M. The telephone rang about seven times before a lady answered in a sleepy British voice. Jim knew Sandra was sharing an apartment with a lady called Agnes Fotheringham and that was probably who answered the telephone.

Jim asked for Sandra.

"I hope you realize it's 3 A.M. here. We British don't enjoy having our sleep disrupted."

"This is an emergency call to my wife."

Jim heard Sandra's voice within half a minute.

"Is that you, Jim?" She, too, sounded very sleepy.

"Were you sucking his cock? Was he giving it to you in the ass?" Jim's speech was slurred due to the drinks he had consumed. He was hurling the vitriolic questions at her in a sobbing voice.

"What are you talking about, Jim?" Sandra's tone was no longer sleepy. She now sounded perplexed.

"I'm talking about the Norwegian bastard you're engaged to."

"It's 3 A.M. here and you're drunk. Call me at a reasonable time when you're sober." She hung up on him.

Jim shed a few tears then heard the front door slam. Martha had come home. Still weeping, Jim threw himself at his younger sister. Martha hugged him and tried to console him by patting him on the back.

"I want you to sleep with me tonight," Jim said. "I want the warmth of another human being beside me while I try to fall asleep. Linus needs a security blanket."

The siblings shared the same bed. Because of all the drinks he had consumed, Jim thought he would not have any difficulty in falling asleep.

However, his agitated mind kept him awake. He kept staring at the ceiling while Martha dozed off. He thought about his sister's recent loss and how it was ironic that they would both be deprived of their "significant other" at the same time. One because of death and the other because of deception. Around 2 A.M. Martha woke up to use the toilet. When she came back she noticed that Jim was wide awake.

"Okay," Martha said. "Get up and let's go jogging."

"Jogging? Are you out of your mind?"

Jim looked at the alarm clock. It was seven minutes after 2 A.M. Greenwich Mean Time was six hours ahead so it was too late to call the bitch in London since she always left home at 7:45 A.M. to catch the underground to get to school. He cursed himself for not calling her sooner. And why hadn't she called him now that she knew her goose was cooked?

Jim and Martha jogged in the tranquility of Memorial Park for a good hour. Despite the fact that he was hung over, Jim was aiming doggedly to keep in step with his young and physically fit sister. He breathed rapidly, almost panting, and his jogging outfit was soaked with perspiration. Martha never made an attempt to slow down nor did she even ask Jim if he needed a rest. Jim was muttering "that fucking bitch" repeatedly as if the words consoled him during the physical challenge he was in.

"Way to go, bro," Martha said. "Get it off your fucking chest!"

When they were finished jogging, Martha was ready to drive back to the house. Jim, however, stretched his hand on a tree and breathed heavily for three minutes. That was the only time he revealed to his sister that he was not physically at a par with her.

"Are you all right, Jim?" Martha asked.

"Sure, Vamanos!"

When they got home Jim threw himself on his own bed, still wearing his jogging outfit, while Martha retreated to her room. This time it did not take too long for Jim to fall asleep. He dozed off as soon as his head touched the pillow and did not wake up until he heard the telephone ring. He looked at his clock radio and discovered it was 3 P.M. He must have slept for ten hours.

"May I speak to Mr. Blackburn?"

He recognized the clipped British voice. It was Agnes Fotheringham. Surely the bitch was not asking her roommate to do the dirty work for her? Did she not have the guts to call him herself?

"This is Jim Blackburn," he replied.

"Mr. Blackburn, this is Agnes Fotheringham."

"Okay, Ms. Fotheringham. Now tell me what she told you to say. Sock it to me!"

There was a long silence. Agnes Fotheringham must have been having second thoughts about being a go-between. The silence was so long that Jim was ready to hang up the telephone. However, he heard her voice again before he had a chance to fulfill this act of arrogance.

"Mr. Blackburn, I got your telephone number from Sandra's address book. I hate to be the one to give you some bad news." Agnes' voice had turned dry and foreboding.

Jim felt like telling her a certain Captain Bruland had beat her to it. If she was calling him to add salt to his wounds, he was ready to shock her proper British ears with a few well-chosen expletives.

"There's been an accident, Mr. Blackburn. A train derailment. Sandra was listed among the thirty-two people who perished. She had taken the underground to get to school."

Jim could see his hand shaking as he held the telephone. As in an impulse he laid the receiver down. He felt emotionally incapable of handling the situation. He could still hear Agnes Fotheringham's faint voice coming from the telephone but was too dazed and shocked to carry on a conversation with her. However, he could decipher what she was saying. She was making reference to a British tragedy that could not have happened at a worse time. The nation was still mourning the death of Princess Diana. After a few minutes it was obvious that Agnes realized that Jim was unwilling to talk to her. He heard her voice asking, "Mr. Blackburn, are you still there?"

Then an open line as if she had hung up the telephone.

At that moment Jim wished Martha was with him. His world was crumbling. Suddenly he began to recall the pleasant memories he had of Sandra. How she helped make the business grow and how she stood by him when Kevin died and later on when he went through an alcohol-related depression. He completely erased the bitterness she brought to him being deceitful. He thought he had made the right decision in leaving Brittany for her. Sandra had been a good wife.

The telephone was off the hook. With a still-shaking hand, Jim grabbed it and dialed his office number. When Martha came on the line he begged her to come home.

"Linus needs another security blanket. Please, please hurry."

"What's wrong, Jim?" Martha asked.

"I'll tell you when you get here," Jim said. He paused then added, "Watch your driving, Martha. I love you and I don't want anything to happen to you. You're all I have left."

Jim gave Martha power of attorney so she could go to London to make arrangements for Sandra's remains to be brought to the States. He was too much of a broken man to go there himself. When Martha returned she told Jim he had gone to Agnes Fotheringham's flat to retrieve Sandra's clothes and other belongings. Sandra had given him a letter addressed to Jim with a PERSONAL and CONFIDENTIAL notation on it.

Dear Mr. Blackburn:

I should first send you my sincere sympathy for your moment of sorrow. There's nothing worse in life, in my opinion, than losing somebody you really loved.

The main reason for writing to you is to assure you that Sandra deeply cared for you until the very end. When you called her in the middle of the night (or should I say the morning?) she had long been separated from her Scandinavian fiancée. He had bedazzled her with expensive gifts and first class trips to Oslo that she felt obligated to tell him she was interested in marrying him.

After he had suggested a Mediterranean cruise on his yacht, Sandra came to her senses and realized the tangled web she had woven. She had lied to him about her marital status and felt bad about it. More than anything, she felt truly rotten about the manner in which she had deceived you.

The night you called and woke us up, she could not go back to sleep. She cried and cried and drowned her sorrow with alcohol.

Mr. Blackburn, Sandra loved you. Please find it in your heart to forgive her for her indiscretion.

Faithfully yours,
Agnes Fotheringham

Sandra was buried in the same burial grounds as Kevin.

CHAPTER NINE

The new millennium began at the stroke of midnight on January 1, 2000. Some had theorized that it would take an additional year to officially welcome the new century, but for all practical purposes the birth of the year 2000 was celebrated around the world as a period of mirthful celebration. People's eyes were glued on their TV sets waiting for the stroke of midnight in cities such as Auckland, Sydney, Beijing, Hong Kong, London, Paris, Rome, and New York. It appeared as if every country on the globe was competing for the most extravagant fireworks display. However, the dawning of the twenty-first century had also promoted fears of catastrophe. Computers were predicted to be affected by the Y2K bug and that would have a negative impact on the general lifestyle. People were urged to store a lot of bottled water, candles, and matches to prepare for the hour of gloom. Some were afraid to fly at the stroke of midnight, thinking that the plane would crash, and religious maniacs were flocking to Jerusalem to be in the Holy City during doomsday. But none of these predictions materialized.

Jim was fifty-nine years old at the birth of the year 2000. He had bought a two-story home in the Clear Lake/NASA suburb of Houston very close to the Johnson Space Center. He owned a motorboat, which he moored at the marina across from where he was living and would often circle the lake to go fishing or just relaxing for hours in a serene environment.

Jim gave a party to celebrate the new millennium and at the stroke of midnight, guests had gathered in the Jacuzzi to watch the fireworks across from the lake.

Marcella Price, a redhead in her late thirties, was there greeting the guests as if she were the mistress of the estate. Marcella was Jim's mistress but not of his estate. She bore a striking resemblance to Sandra but intellectually she did not measure up to Jim's late wife. She was simply his subservient mistress and Jim was grateful to her for accepting her role in his life. He called her his "redneck redhead" and she called him her "gorgeous sugar daddy." Marcella was just content in giving Jim his sexual favors whenever he asked for them as long as she could flaunt the jewelry he gave her at the life insurance company where she worked.

Martha was also at the party. She was now forty-four years old and she brought her "significant other" with her to the party. Tara was only eighteen years old and seemed to be very much in love with Martha. She clung to her older lover like a vine. Jim teased Martha about robbing the cradle and Martha told him that he had no room to talk since he was shacking up with that younger flaming redhead.

The guests, including the flaming redhead, left around 2 A.M. Jim had asked Martha and Tara to stay overnight. They decided to circle the lake by boat and took a liter of Glennfidich Scotch with them, which they drank out of the bottle. They could still hear some of the New Year's Eve revelers as they circled the lake. When it was time to dock the boat, Jim asked Martha to throw the mooring line on the buoy since he was too drunk and tired to do it himself.

Jim passed out as soon as he hit the bed. He woke up around 2 P.M. and was surprised to find out that he had slept for almost eleven hours. He had a hangover and felt a sense of fatigue that he had never experienced before in his life. He smelled the aroma of bacon being fried. Obviously, Martha and Tara were cooking an afternoon breakfast. Jim felt weak and dizzy and held on to the banister as he walked down the stairs to the lower level. Halfway down the staircase, he tumbled to the ground. Still conscious, he could see Martha and Tara rush to assist him. He told them not to worry. It was just a hangover and all he needed was aspirin and coffee. However, Martha insisted that he see a doctor and drove him to St. John's Hospital in Clear Lake. Martha told Tara to stay behind as if she wanted to be alone with her brother in his moment of distress.

At the Emergency Room of St. John's Hospital, Jim was asked if he had a private physician whom they should contact. He was insured by Cigna Healthcare Systems, who had appointed Dr. Sam Richardson as his physician. The old doctor, however, had retired and Jim had procrastinated in asking Cigna to assign him a new physician. He had not had a physical examination in over a year and could not give the name of his current doctor. They took his blood pressure and temperature at the emergency room. His blood pressure was normal but he was running a fever of 102 degrees Fahrenheit. As they could not diagnose his symptoms, they asked him to stay at the hospital overnight for blood tests. Jim asked Martha to go back home and he would call her in the morning once they had the results of the tests. He retired in a private hospital room after the tests but had a hard time falling asleep that night. He had a serious case of the chills and his teeth were clattering incessantly. He called for help and a nurse came and took his temperature. It was still very high and she came back with two Tylenol tablets and an ice pack. Gradually the chills and shakes had diminished and he was able to fall asleep.

The next morning he was visited by a tall, skeletal Indian doctor named Ravi Dalvi.

"The news is not too jolly," the doctor said. "The blood tests show that you are suffering from some form of cancer. Either leukemia or lymphoma."

"Cancer?" Jim could not believe what he was hearing. "Does that mean I'm going to die?"

"Aren't we all going to die?"

Jim did not know whether to take that as a positive or negative response. The doctor went on to tell him that he would have to undergo a bone marrow extraction. He could perform it himself since he was a hematologist. It would involve sticking two very long needles in the buttocks area and using a lot of pressure to remove a bone marrow sample. Jim asked him if it would be painful.

"Mind over matter," said Dr. Dalvi. "Mind over matter. We will, of course, numb the area before doing the extraction. It will be similar to having a tooth pulled out."

The procedure was to be done that afternoon. Jim felt like calling Martha to sneak in some scotch in a small camping bottle but quickly abandoned the idea. It was too great a risk to take. His sister might get caught by the hospital staff. But he did call Martha.

"They found out I have cancer," Jim said in a dry voice.

It took less than fifteen minutes for Martha to be by his side weeping and embracing him. This time she was accompanied by Tara.

"Don't ever give up," Martha said. "Please don't give up. For my sake."

Later on Martha and Tara were asked to leave the room so Dr. Dalvi could perform his bone marrow extraction. Jim tried not to think of the giant needles being inserted in him. The pressure was tremendous but the pain was similar to hurting one's funny bone. He did not know whether to laugh or cry. Within ten minutes, Dr. Dalvi showed him the tiny bone he had extracted just like a dentist would show his patient a tooth he had pulled.

"See, I told you. Mind over matter," said the doctor.

The next morning Jim was told that the bone marrow sample definitely revealed that he had non-Hodgkin's Lymphoma, a cancer characterized by progressive enlargement of the lymph nodes. Chances of survival after chemotherapy or radiation were only 25 percent. He would have had a better chance of conquering the cancer had he just had Hodgkin's Lymphoma, but luck was not on his side, and x-rays also showed that he had been stricken with the deadlier malignancy. Dr. Dalvi advised him that his insurance was accepted at the MD Anderson Cancer Center and he had made arrangements for him to be treated there.

The University of Texas MD Anderson Cancer Center near downtown Houston is reputed to be the best in the world for the treatment of cancer. The equipment and research that they use in conquering the malady is, with no exaggeration, unsurpassed. People from all over the United States and the world flock there for their treatment. The conglomeration of races at the center is comparable to what one sees at the United Nations building. Even the television channels in the patients' rooms broadcast in such foreign languages as Spanish, Arabic, Korean, and Chinese. MD Anderson is called a center but in reality it is a very sophisticated hospital that opens its doors to the hapless afflicted with cancer regardless of age, sex, or race.

But MD Anderson is not devoid of flaws. Jim became a patient at a time when the nation was facing a serious shortage of professional medical staff. Doctors were dropping the profession because of the numerous malpractice suits, and because of advances made in the women's liberation movement, female college graduates were not choosing nursing as a career. They were more attracted to becoming architects, lawyers, and policewomen where the pay was better and they did not have to empty bedpans. At cane time Filipino nurses were in abundance. But now even they were becoming scarce. The government of the Philippines had restricted nurses from moving to other countries because of the dire need for their profession at home. These shortages of medical staff caused patients to sometimes wait over three hours to have someone attend to them. Signs stating WAIT WATCHERS—PLEASE ADVISE US IF YOU FEEL YOU HAVE WAITED TOO LONG were of little use.

At MD Anderson, Jim was assigned Dr. Maria Guerrero to be his primary care physician. On his first visit, he waited for two hours before a physician assistant called his name. He was examined by the physician assistant then waited another hour for Dr. Guerrero. Jim was accompanied by Marcella Price and they both did not see the point in contradicting those who assumed she was Mrs. Blackburn. He had another bone marrow extraction prior to meeting Dr. Guerrero and since the bandage became loose, he had blood all over his trousers. Jim asked Marcella to go to the nearest K-Mart to buy him a pair of gym pants. In the meantime, they loaned him a hospital frock to wear when he saw Dr. Guerrero.

Dr. Maria Guerrero was in her mid-fifties and of Latino heritage. She spoke English with no accent and Jim assumed her roots were either Spanish or Argentine. The first thing she told Jim was that he was a very sick man. She suggested a spleen removal since a lot of the cancer was concentrated around the spleen area. After that she recommended nine sessions of chemotherapy with twenty-one-day intervals between each session. The chemotherapy was to be done at the hospital or at home with a portable pump, depending on her decision. Each chemotherapy session would take at least forty-eight hours.

Dr. Guerrero went on to describe to Jim the effects of chemotherapy. The chances of losing his hair and a tremendous amount of weight were 90 percent but some people did not experience the other effects of the treatment such as nausea or mouth blisters. Chemotherapy would destroy the cancer cells but affect some of the other body elements, such as magnesium, thus giving the patient anemia and fatigue.

"I see you're single," said Dr. Guerrero. "Does that mean you live alone?"

"Yes, that is correct."

"This might create a problem since I do not recommend driving. Chemotherapy usually makes one uncoordinated."

She continued to tell Jim that he would have to come to the hospital twice a week to have his blood drawn and be examined by a physician assistant. Every so often he would have to undergo CAT scans, x-rays, and bone marrow extractions. He would also have to take his temperature every day and when it was over 101 degrees Fahrenheit, he would have to immediately come to the emergency room, regardless of the time of day or night.

Jim was concentrating on means to solve the driving problem instead of fully absorbing what the doctor was telling him. He had employed a Mexican housekeeper to clean his home twice a week and was now thinking of asking her if she could be his driver when he required it. He quickly scrapped the idea. He had seen Lupe clumsily manage her car in his driveway and the bumps on her fenders demonstrated that she was a reckless driver. Of course he could also ask Martha to temporarily move in with him and he would not object to his bringing Tara along. And how about Marcella Price? She could really demonstrate her gratitude to her sugar daddy. She owed it to him. He also eliminated these ideas. Jim Blackburn was too independent to rely on the favors of others. If he needed a driver or a "Man Friday," he could afford hiring one. He would prefer paying for a service than feeling obligated to the charitable acts of those close to him. Jim was a self-made man, almost an island.

"Mr. Blackburn?" Dr. Guerrero seemed to have become aware that her patient had drifted into another world. "Do you hear what I'm saying?"

"Yes doctor, I hear you well."

"You're a very sick man, Mr. Blackburn. I strongly recommend that you prepare a will for your loved ones and make amends to those in your life whom you have hurt. You can also prepare a Living Will so your relatives can allow the life support systems to cease when all hope is gone."

These words truly knocked him off his daze. The doctor was handing him a death sentence. He recalled the days when physicians would not reveal to patients that their days were numbered and wondered if the present approach was proper. And what right did she have to tell him to make amends to others? Did she ever make amends to her patients for scaring the shit out of them? He left her office with an inner feeling that he would not enjoy having that woman as a doctor.

At the waiting room, Jim saw a sight comparable to a Felini surrealistic movie. Marcella Price was sitting there holding a K-Mart bag and fraternizing with a midget. He must have told her a joke because she was laughing hysterically. She introduced him as Mr. Abraham Lerner and he jumped off his seat and extended his little hand to Jim. He sported a gray beard and his face was heavily wrinkled. He explained that he, too, was a patient of Dr. Guerrero. They talked for a few minutes about the chemotherapy treatment and before they separated, the midget told Jim, "Don't let that heartless doctor scare you. She's just a religious nut and a prophet of doom. As long as there's life, there's hope. Remember that a Jewish leprechaun told you that."

Jim changed into the gym pants Marcella had bought him before they left MD Anderson Cancer Center.

Ten days later, he underwent the spleen removal surgery. He was told that it was necessary to stop smoking for at least a week before the operation. He had been a heavy smoker for forty years and tried to quit several times with no avail. Thus he thought that abandoning the cancer sticks would be an ordeal. It turned out not to be too hard. He bought nicotine patches and tolerated the withdrawal symptoms with ease. His mind was too occupied thinking about his cancer and the spleen removal he was to experience. Since he was told he would be losing weight rapidly, he was not worried about the pounds he would gain while he tried to quit smoking.

The spleen removal turned out to be successful. Jim woke up seeing a woman with her head covered by a Muslim "abaya" scarf. He thought he had died and gone to heaven. Maybe Islam was God's chosen religion after all. He quickly perished the thought when he saw his sister Martha standing next to her. When she left, Martha told him she was a Muslim refugee nurse from Cosovo. Since the Filipino nurses could no longer be recruited, MD Anderson was hiring ethnic Albanian nurses from the troubled area in the former Yugoslavia.

Martha also told Jim that she had spoken to the doctor who performed the surgery and found out that they removed two spleens instead of one. One spleen was only as big as his thumb. Jim was not aware that he was a biological rarity. Martha stayed with her brother all afternoon and they discussed what steps should be taken to ensure that he would not be a risk at home while he was undergoing the chemotherapy treatment. Martha had heard of an alarm necklace that Jim could wear and all he had to do was press the button if he felt he needed help. He had already ordered it and they would install the special telephone at Jim's home as soon as he got out of the hospital. They also found a solution to the driving problem. Jim would not need to hire a private chauffeur. A transportation company called Danners, Inc., that they used to take crewmembers from the ships to hospitals, airport, etc., could be used to drive him to MD Anderson whenever the need arose. They were open twenty-four hours a day and could make it to Jim's home in less than half an hour after he called them. Therefore, stubborn Jim, who did not want to depend on others, could still live by himself and take the necessary safety measures while he was under treatment.

Then came the matter of the will. Jim advised Martha to see an attorney as soon as possible. Martha was to be the executor of his estate. She was to inherit the business and most of the rest of his assets, including his home in Clear Lake. Brittany, who was still living in Rhode Island, was to get $100,000, Marcella Price, $25,000; and Lupe the part-time housekeeper, $10,000. $10,000 was to be donated to his favorite charity, the Disabled American Veterans, and all his wardrobe was to be given to Goodwill Industries. Jim was determined not to leave anything to his son Rodney, whom he had long ago disowned. He had heard that Rodney had become an architect and was living in San Francisco with his wife and two sons. Jim was ignoring his grandchildren because of their father's transgression.

Before receiving the first chemotherapy treatment, Jim had to experience the very painful procedure of having a catheter inserted in his chest. The right vein had to be found to attach the tubular device. It was imperative to have it done so that he could receive the anti-cancer drugs intravenously. He compared the pain to the catheter they had attached to his penis at a Vietnamese hospital when he was wounded. Jim suddenly used a spiritual approach to the pain by thinking of the passions of Christ when He was having nails inserted in the palms of His hands. He had not practiced organized religion in ages but that was a moment when he badly needed a soothing crutch. At the end of the tubing they added two punctured caps which they called sutures. Jim was to replace the sutures himself every two weeks and have the large bandage attaching the sutures to the tubing changed by the hospital staff every ten days.

The first chemotherapy treatment went smoothly. He was hospitalized for fifty-five hours and had his eyes fixed on the television set while he had the anticancer drugs slowly penetrate his body intravenously. The most bothersome part was that they included a medicine that made him want to urinate endlessly for the first half-hour and he had to jump out of bed with the IV equipment attached to his tubing to use the urine bottle. He had to record the amount of liquids he drank and report it to the nurse so she could compare it to what was disposed of in the urine bottle. Like a VCR, input and output was the name of the game. Input and rapid output also affected what he ate. The chemotherapy irritated the lining of his intestines and robbed him of magnesium. Hence they had to include magnesium with what was injected in his catheter and that gave him diarrhea as he had never felt before in his life. Rushing to the toilet while dragging the IV equipment was a difficult task and sometimes he would inadvertently pull on the sutures, causing a lot of pain. On one occasion, he had to push the call button and with embarrassment to advise the nurse that he needed to have his sheets and hospital gown changed since he shat all over himself. He asked for anti-diarrhea pills but that constipated him. He could not win for losing.

Shortly after the first chemotherapy, Jim started losing weight rapidly. His appetite diminished every day and he found it a burden to have an ordinary meal. At advice of the hospital dietician, he compensated for the lack of food by drinking diet supplements. He was not allowed to eat raw fruit and vegetables because of the chemicals used in these food groups. Day by day, his immunity weakened and he became susceptible to colds and chills. One night his temperature rose to 103 degrees Fahrenheit and he was hospitalized for three weeks. He had contacted pneumonia. He found it unusual that doctors at MD Anderson worked in teams when a patient is hospitalized. He therefore did not see Dr. Guerrero since her team did not work in his ward during his stay. One week he had a Turkish and a Colombian doctor; the next week a Swedish doctor and an American of Armenian descent; and the third week, an Italian woman doctor and an aristocratic Dutchman who spoke like a Brit. The United Nations factor prevailed even among the physicians at MD Anderson.

Dr. Guerro allowed him to have the second chemotherapy at home. He carried a strapped portable pump with tubes attached to his chest catheter. Carrying the big contraption was bothersome and he could not decide if it was better than being pinned in a hospital bed. He could notice his hair thinning and sometimes felt blisters inside his mouth. He would spend time in front of a mirror to scrutinize his deteriorating self. He was losing weight and his cheekbones were beginning to protrude. Jim was not a man of cliches but he could not help asking himself repeatedly, "Why me?"

Once again he was zapped by a spiritual feeling and found comfort by going to his computer and typing some answers to his question.

"Why me? Because I am a child of God and like all of God's children, I am given only a temporary stay in this beautiful domain."

"Why me? Because I feel I have led a full life. Like everybody else, I had my ups and downs, but with God's help I was able to persevere and endure. I am most grateful to my Maker for the sister he gave me and the wonderful friendship bonds I made with people of different races and lifestyles. For those who have left the earth before me, I look forward to our loving reunion with excitement. Those who will follow me, I will greet with the hugs and embraces that we are so accustomed to."

"Why me? Because God has chosen that this is the time for me to go to the next abode. I am packing my bags as I did during my trips to interesting countries of the world. This time my bags are packed for the most outstanding of all places. The knowledge I will acquire alone makes me anxious to get there.”

Having had his spiritual moment, he then resorted to drinking heavily without really caring if the mixture of alcohol and the strong anti-cancer drugs he was pumping into his body would be detrimental to his health. In fact, deep down he was hoping the grim reaper would pay him a visit. That way, those close to him would call it alcohol poisoning instead of suicide. And who would blame him for overdrinking in his condition? He was not going to take the pseudo-macho option that Ernest Hemingway took and shoot himself. Hemingway, the epitome of manliness, had ended his life in a pusil-lanimous manner since he proved he was too weak to live and fight his can-cer. With him it would be an accidental death and like Errol Flynn, he would die with a smile on his face. He also thought of Yolanda, the whore who eventually died of an overdose. Maybe Yolanda was now performing oral sex on Errol Flynn in hell. That thought served as a comedic relief and he burst out laughing.

The combination of drugs and alcohol did not kill Jim. The days turned into weeks then months. He would get chemotherapy treatments at the hos-pital and at home every twenty-one days and sometimes his blood and platelet levels were extremely low, so he would need transfusions. Sometimes he would also get dehydrated and would have large amounts of liquids inject-ed through the catheter. After his fifth chemotherapy treatment he had lost all his hair and shed forty pounds. Whenever his temperature rose, he would call Danners, Inc., to rush him to the hospital. Since he could not control his urine, he would carry a bottle with him and relieve himself in the van.

Martha and Tara would often spend the night at his Jim’s home but his relationship with Marcella had soured. Whether it was physical or emotion-al, he felt his sexual drive had diminished and he would go through a lot of exertion to reach an orgasm. He was going to inquire about his condition allowing him to take a new pill on the market called Viagra, which enhanced a man’s sexual potency. However he dropped the idea. As his malady had made him abstain from cigarettes, he could also learn how to abstain from sex. He had to make adjustments during his battle with the dreaded disease. Marcella gracefully exited from his life.

After his ninth chemotherapy session, Jim was advised that he would have to undergo another three since MD Anderson had successfully experi-mented with new drugs. He was told that if the drugs did not work, he might have to consider radiation.

On one of his visits to Dr. Guerrero, he had some blood drawn and the bandage came loose, leaving a bloody mess on his shirt sleeve. Margaret, the doctor’s Jamaican nurse, made him remove his shirt so she could wash it in the sink.

"And what shall I wear?" Jim asked.

"I'll lend you a hospital shirt."

Jim agreed to let her wash his shirt but twenty minutes later while he was in the doctor's waiting room, Margaret came back with tears in her eyes. His shirt was burnt to a crisp.

"I put it in the microwave to let it dry quickly," she sobbed.

"Thanks for adding humor to my day," said Jim. "I needed that."

He did indeed need humor to prepare him for Dr. Guerrero. He could not help but recall the little Jewish "leprechaun" calling her a prophet of doom. Not one smile was cracked as she advised him about the new drugs he would be given on his next chemotherapy. Should they succeed in destroying most of the cancer cells, he had to think about a bone marrow transplant. It was a very costly procedure but she thought his insurance would pay for most of it if they could prove that this was the last resort. Of course, if the chemotherapy did not destroy most of the cancer cells, they would have to try radiation.

"Who are your living relatives?" Dr. Guerrero asked.

"Just my sister Martha."

"Good. Tell her she will have to be tested to see if he can be a suitable donor."

The doctor continued to tell him that if his physical condition after the third chemotherapy permitted it, a donor would not be required. They could remove his own bone marrow, have it purified, and then reinserted in his body. To do this, he would have to have the right quantities of red blood cells and platelets.

Martha had her blood drawn. Tests results proved that her blood type could not make her a suitable bone marrow donor. Furthermore, after the third chemotherapy, Jim was told that his physical condition did not allow them to use his own bone marrow for the transplant. He had to have a donor.

CHAPTER TEN

Dr. Samer Helmi was from Cairo, Egypt. His well-to-do parents had made him attend the local American school since he was a child with the intention of having him further his studies in the United States when he reached the college level. He won a scholarship at Rice University and later enrolled at the Baylor School of Medicine. After he became a physician, he married a Texan woman who converted to his Islamic faith and settled in Houston in spite of his parents' insistence that he return to Cairo and serve his people. Dr. Helmi had become Americanized. He seemed to be very devoted to his profession and gained respect from his patients and peers at MD Anderson's Bone Marrow Transplantation section. Unlike Dr. Guerrero, he encouraged his patients to think positively. Before Jim left his clinic, Dr. Helmi told him, "Keep telling yourself that like the Allstate people, you're in good hands."

Jim was to carry a beeper with him at all times so he could be notified when a donor with an "O" blood type was located.

When he got home, Jim received a telephone call that was like a ray from the past. He recognized Brittany's voice and was stunned by the fact that his former wife would call him after so many years. She was quick and to the point. Jim's mother had heard from Martha about his condition. She knew that Martha was not a suitable donor so she was offering him Rodney's telephone number in San Francisco. She had spoken to Rodney and stated that their firstborn was willing to have a blood sample taken to see if he could be a suitable donor. Jim was overtaken by his pride and felt like hanging up the telephone. But he thought about the fact that here was a woman whom he had abandoned years ago calling him with good intentions. He told her that she need not give him Rodney's telephone number. He was not going to call him.

Brittany began to sermonize. She talked at a fast pace, reminding him that he had almost ruined Rodney's life by making him go on a guilt trip over an unfortunate accident. Rodney had to go through extensive psychological treatment to rid himself of the traumatic moment of that one night. He was now happily married and a parent. He yearned for Jim's forgiveness and blessing.

He wanted desperately to save Jim's life to make up for taking Kevin's life. Jim's pride once again took over his emotions. He compromised by asking Brittany to have Rodney call him. But he was not going to call Rodney.

Jim heard Rodney's voice on the telephone twenty-four hours later. There was a long pause after he said the word "Dad" as if he was waiting for his father's reaction.

"Is that you, Rodney?" Jim asked.

"Yes, Dad, I'm here in Houston."

Jim felt compelled to make conversation.

"When did you get here?"

"About an hour ago. I'm staying at the Clear Lake Hilton, which, I am told, is only a five minutes drive to your home."

Jim suddenly swallowed his pride.

"Come on over, son."

Rodney was now thirty-seven years old. Jim had forgotten that his son had inherited his looks and now seeing him as an adult was like seeing a cloned version of himself. The two men embraced and wept in each other's arms.

"I'm here with you now, Dad," Rodney said. "I will not rest until you are in complete remission."

They had a seafood dinner at the Kemah boardwalk and Rodney told his father about his family in San Francisco. He was married to Trisha, a school teacher, and had two sons, James Leonard, eight, and Robert Kevin, six. Jim and Rodney seemed to have made an unspoken agreement not to talk about the departed Kevin. However, Jim couldn't help but wonder why Rodney's second son had Kevin as a middle name. He assumed that if Rodney gave his son Kevin as a first name it would conjure up bitter memories on a daily basis. He must have settled for Kevin as a middle name since he cared for his brother and found a means of dedication. The name Kevin would be a permanent imprint on his son's birth records. Jim looked at the photos of Rodney's family. Trisha was a blue-eyed beauty with golden hair. The older boy James looked a lot like her but Robert did not look like either of his parents. However, the six-year-old did look familiar to Jim. He looked just like his uncle Kevin.

Rodney checked out of his room at the Hilton and spent the night with his father. The next morning, they went to MD Anderson so Rodney could have a blood test. Dr. Helmi was surprised to know that Jim had a son and reprimanded him for putting his life at risk by playing with time. When the results of Rodney's blood test proved that he would be a suitable donor for his father, Dr. Helmi dismissed any criticism of Jim and with a broad smile on his face gave the two men the good news. Jim and his son once again hugged each other and shed tears of joy.

A week later, they reported to MD Anderson for the transplant. Jim had hoped they could share the same room for the transplant and converse during the transfer of bone marrow. This, however, was not possible since all the patients' rooms at MD Anderson were built for single occupancy.

Although the transplant had cost Jim's insurance over $200,000 it was surprisingly simple and quick. To intravenously remove Rodney's bone marrow took two hours and to inject it into Jim's veins another two hours. It was done at a time when tropical storm Allison had devastated the Houston Medical area and they had to spend two useless nights at MD Anderson because the inclement weather made it impossible to drive back to Jim's home in Clear Lake. Rodney made Jim promise that he would visit him and his family in San Francisco as soon as he was healthy enough to travel by plane.

However, that trip had to be postponed. The toils of chemotherapy had weakened Jim's body to the extent that he had a mild heart attack, ironically while he was being visited by Dr. Helmi. He was not aware of what was going on except that he heard the doctor say "I'm losing him," then saw a couple of nurses rushing to his room. He was later told that he had a very close call. He also suffered from dehydration and would regularly come to the clinic to have liquids pumped into his system.

Three months after the bone marrow transplant, Jim had a stroke. He was at home by himself one evening and had come out of the shower when he slipped and fell. He experienced numbness on his left side and was unable to get up. To make things worse, he had removed the alarm button from his chest, not wanting to have it wet when he took his shower. He had been told that water would not damage the gadget but his stubborn fantasy of being electrocuted made him remove it. Jim lay on the wet floor naked. His head was on the hard bathroom tile and he was unable to get up and answer the telephone in his bedroom. He could hear Rodney's voice on the voice mail. It seemed like his son was calling him at least every twenty minutes. After the fourth call he sounded very frantic.

"Dad, please, please call. I'm starting to worry."

Jim hit his head on the tile floor after he failed to get up and answer the telephone. He shut his eyes and felt a dizziness invading his mind. Suddenly, he had the urge to pray. He quickly repeated The Lord's Prayer several times then switched to Hail Marys. He passed out after he said the words of a prayer he had learned in Catholic schools. He remembered the prayer being called "Salve Regina." He mumbled the words he could recall:

"Hail Holy Queen, Mother of Mercy. Hail our life, our sweetness, and our hope. To thee do we cry, poor banished children of Eve. To thee do we send out our sighs, mourning and weeping in this valley of tears."

Jim was awakened by Martha gently shaking him. He was soaking in his own urine and had no sensation in his left arm. He could barely make out what Martha was saying. However, an ambulance and paramedics arrived shortly thereafter so it was obvious that Martha had called 911. Jim could hear the ambulance driver and paramedic talking as he lay on the stretcher. They were referring to the fact that he had been lying on his cold bathroom floor for eighteen hours. He would have died if his son in San Francisco had not called his sister in Houston, who had a key to his house. Jim spent the night at St. John's Hospital in Clear Lake then was transferred to MD Anderson in the morning. The stroke had not affected his speech but he still had difficulty moving this left arm.

Jim fell asleep and was later awakened by the sound of whispers. He opened his eyes and found himself surrounded by Rodney, Martha, and Tara. The three were wearing surgical masks and rubber gloves in compliance with the clinic's regulations. Jim had never seen his son and sister in the same room and suddenly remembered Rodney's homophobia. He was grateful to his son for being there and was hoping that he had genuinely accepted his aunt's lifestyle and not putting on a phony act to please his father.

"Hey, y' all," Jim said.

"You're lucky to be alive," Martha said. "It's Rodney's devotion to you that saved you."

With teary eyes, Jim extended his right hand to his visitors and they took turns in embracing him. This was the weakest moment in his life. Never had he had such a need for people to help him. Never had he been so grateful to others for being there when he needed them. They stayed with him a full hour. Rodney had to fly back to San Francisco the next morning but he promised that he would call on a daily basis.

"I'm leaving him in your good hands," he told Martha.

As they were getting ready to leave, the physician on duty examined Jim and advised that his stay at the clinic would probably be a lengthy one since he would have to undergo physical therapy to regain the strength in his left arm. Martha and Tara assured him that they would check on his mail. Martha would also pay his bills since he had given her check signing authority.

Nurse Martina Cosey was in her early thirties and the most beautiful African-American woman Jim had ever laid his eyes on. She walked into Jim's room after the others left and introduced herself as the nurse on duty. She told him that the physician had suggested that he wear a condom catheter, which would prevent him from getting up and using the toilet to urinate. The word "catheter" brought painful memories and he told her he'd rather keep getting up if it meant being tortured. Martina laughed and explained to him that this "catheter" was not painful. It was a condom with a tube attached to a sac that would store the urine. Martina was to insert his penis in the condom but he could always ask for a male nurse to do it if he was bashful.

"What can I say," Jim said since he could not think of anything to say. He quickly added, "Of course, I'm not bashful. You seem to be very efficient in all aspects of your profession."

He had stuck his foot in his mouth and it made her giggle.

"It's all in the name of medicine, Mr. Blackburn," she said.

After she had inserted the condom catheter she told Jim, "With patience and the proper treatment, you'll soon be out and about."

"Are you from Maryland?" Jim asked.

"Maryland? Do I speak with a drawl?"

"Just the way you pronounced 'out and about'."

"I'm from Windsor, Ontario, Canada, a few miles north of Detroit, Michigan."

"Canada, eh?" Jim said trying to sound Canadian.

"Yes, Canada. Most people find it hard to believe that black people live in the frozen north. I guess they think that we can only tolerate hot climates. My parents immigrated from Jamaica."

"With a name like Martina, I would think they immigrated from an Eastern European country."

"I was named after Dr. Martin Luther King. My twin brother, Martin, died at childbirth."

~ ~ ~

It did not take long for Martina to become Jim's favorite nurse. Although he hated being incapacitated, it was a consolation to him to depend on someone with a big heart and pleasing attitude. She helped him take his daily shower, changed his sheets when he had bladder or bowel "accidents," and since he had lost his appetite, she made sure he ordered diet supplement drinks with his meals. Jim dreaded it when Martina was not on duty. She was good for his morale and a boost to his quick recovery. They also developed a friendship bond. He told her about his two marriages but did not mention the Rodney/Kevin tragedy since he had erased it from his mind when he forgave his son. On the other hand, she told him about her failed marriage to a white Texan who brought her to Houston then beat her up when she became pregnant with his daughter. He could not control his liquor and would call her a "nigger bitch" when he was in a drunken stupor. She showed Jim a photo of her eleven-year-old girl. Melanie was fair-skinned and Martina mentioned the challenges she faced being raised by a single black mother.

"It's she and I against the world, but we are there for each other."

Jim spent a total of four months at MD Anderson, recovering from his stroke. He would undergo physical therapy twice a day and he regained some strength on his left arm and leg. However, he felt some numbness and tingling in his feet which necessitated him to walk with a cane. Before being released from the clinic, he was told that he would have to have a qualified person care for him when he was at home. Martina was the first person to cross his mind and he approached her about being his live-in nurse. He would show her as an employee of Blackburn Shipping Agency and her salary would be over $50,000, which was much more than what she earned at MD Anderson. Martina politely declined.

"I'm thinking of my little girl," she said. "Being a live-in nurse would separate her from me."

"How careless of me to forget about Melanie," Jim said. "You can bring her with you. I've got lots of room and she can be enrolled at a school in Clear Lake where she can mingle with children of astronauts and NASA scientists."

"How many of them have a single black parent?" Martina asked.

"I promise you, Martina, now there will be three of us against the world."

Jim's words were prophetic. Some his neighbors and friends started to shun him after Martina and Melanie moved in with him. It was difficult to make them aware of their small minds. Martina was just earning a living. There was nothing sexual or even romantic about their relationship. Martha and Tara would often visit and they would take the boat to circle the lake. Jim considered this a special treat since he was physically too weak to man the boat himself. He enjoyed the fact that Martina and Melanie were able to share one of his passions with him. But people in their boats who, in the past, gleefully waved at them, were now turning their heads the other way.

Since Jim was going through a spiritual awakening, he would have Martina drive him to the nearest Catholic church for mass every Sunday. She would dutifully help him up the stairs and escort him to his seat. Then she would leave and return to pick him up when the service was over. One Sunday he asked her to join him for the entire mass. She stood out as the only black person among the all white conmarthaation. However, she wore a nurse's uniform as if deliberately evoking the image that she was simply there to care for her patient.

Martina introduced Jim to spicy Jamaican cooking and like a drill sergeant she would make sure that he ate every scrap on his plate. She also insisted that he drink eight glasses of water a day under her supervision and limited his alcohol intake to three drinks a day.

"You do want a speedy recovery, eh?" Martina asked.

"Cross my heart I do, eh?" Jim replied.

She and Melanie joined Jim at church the following Sunday and this time he asked her not to wear her uniform.

"Let them think we're a family," Jim said then hummed the tune of "You and I Against the World."

After mass, Jim asked her if she followed any religious denomination.

"I'm a non-practicing Anglican, which is why I can relate to the Catholic service," she said. "Melanie was baptized as an Episcopalian but neither of us attend church, although we do believe in a supreme being."

She went on to tell him that she worked with an Iranian doctor at MD Anderson and he made her take an interest in the Baha'i faith. She stopped attending their meetings since she started working for Jim.

"And why is that?" Jim asked.

"I wanted to devote every minute of my time to serving you."

Jim gave her an affectionate hug and kissed her on the cheek.

"You're too good for your own good," he said.

He then told her that he wanted to attend one of those Baha'i meetings with her.

Dr. Abbas Mahvash remembered Jim as a patient at MD Anderson. Jim, however, did not recall ever seeing him there. He apologized and blamed it on his state of mind while he was being treated. The doctor and his wife Lola owned a beautiful home in League City, Texas, not too far from Clear Lake. They gave a weekly Baha'i "fireside meeting" which included prayer and spiritual discussions followed by a scrumptious Persian dinner. The people attending the meeting were American converts of mixed ethnic origin since race unity played a major part in the Baha'i dogma. There were also many Iranians who had fled their country because of the persecution of their people by the Ayatollah Khomeini. The Mahvash's sixteen-year-old daughter, Amethyst, started the meeting by reading some of the words of Baha'u'llah the prophet who founded the faith in Iran in the late nineteenth century. Amethyst spoke American English with a superb diction that gave a lot of meaning to what she was reading.

"The Baha'i faith really encourages women to obtain a good education," Martina whispered to Jim. "This prepares them to become good mothers."

When Amethyst finished reading, Dr. Mahvash spoke about some of the tenets of the Baha'i religion. The doctor acted as if he were speaking directly to Jim, since he was the only newcomer to the meeting. Dr. Mahvash explained how the faith forbade the creation of a priesthood. All followers participated equally and no power was vested in individuals. Every year, the adult members of each local Baha'i community selected nine community members to serve on a local Spiritual Assembly. The Universal House of Justice in Haifa, Israel, was the main authority for the Baha'i world. There were more than 1200 local spiritual assemblies in the United States and more than 17,000 in the world. Since Baha'u'llah was born a Shiite Muslim, a lot of the Islamic teachings such as yearly fasting and the recognition of all prophets as messengers of God were incorporated in the Baha'i faith. Like Muslims, those of the Baha'i religion were prohibited from drinking alcoholic beverages.

"I guess I could never make a Baha'i," Jim whispered to Marina. "I love my scotch too much. Even the small rations you allow me."

Martina smiled and pressed her hand on his. She didn't let go for a long time. She had made an intimate gesture in front of a group of people and didn't seem to be self-conscious about what they thought about her relationship with Jim. Martina had finally truly shed her nurse's uniform.

When they returned home that evening they found a brief handwritten note on the kitchen counter. Melanie had let her know that she was spending the night at a friend's place. No friend's name or telephone number was given. Martina acted worried and angry.

"I shouldn't have left her by herself," she said.

She then told Jim that Melanie was dependable enough to be left by herself since she was eight years old. Martina's working hours and lack of funds for a sitter compelled her to train her daughter to be unsupervised when the need arose. Since they moved to Clear Lake, Melanie seemed to forget she was a minor. She would not tell her mother of the friends she frequented as if she did not have the right to know.

"She's ashamed of me," Martina said, her voice breaking. "I sometimes wonder if it was wise to expose her to a predominantly white neighborhood."

She started to sob and Jim took her in his arms and gently stroked her hair. As she kept on crying he could feel a certain quiver in her body as if she were sexually aroused. He gently lowered his head on her bosom. His warm kisses were no longer meant to console. She had now stimulated his desires and he was giving in. She allowed him to disrobe her and stood naked in front of him as he undressed himself. He led her to the master bedroom.

"Be tolerant," he whispered. "It's been a while for me."

"My darling," she said. "I could wait a lifetime for this moment."

Jim felt like a man fulfilled. The cancer was a thing of the past. He was alive and well.

CHAPTER ELEVEN

James Blackburn
16231 Santa Rita Street
Houston, Texas 77096
Tel: 713-555-1866
E-Mail: Jim__Blackburn@oceans.net

XMAS 2002

Dear friends:

This is the very first Christmas form letter I have written in my life and I hope you will forgive me if it reaches the point of boredom. Some people, I am told, think that form letters are reserved for the self-centered. Self-centeredness is not where I live. I prefer to be thought of as a blessed braggart expounding on the wonderful year he's had.

I will remember 2002 as my "rainbow year" since a rainbow sometimes follows a storm. Having survived cancer, a spleen removal, a heart attack, a stroke, and a bone marrow transplant, I feel like a walking miracle despite the fact that I now require a cane to walk.

My biggest achievement of the year was my marriage to my new bride, Martina. Martina nursed and nurtured me during the hardest days of my recovery and I thank the good Lord for sending her and her daughter Melanie to me. We had differences at first with Melanie as many parents have with children in their pre-teen years but I feel that we now have a meeting of minds through the love and understanding we all share. Melanie now considers me her dad and I have already taken the first steps to officially adopt her. Our family bond has also been strengthened by our spirituality. Martina has converted to the Baha'i religion and we use the concepts of her new faith in our interracial marriage. As for me, I decided to remain Catholic in worship but unassociated with any organized faith in my private relationship with my Higher Power.

My business is now being run by my beloved sister Martha. Sometimes I miss the maritime world and the subculture involved in it. Once a week I meet with some of my old business cronies for lunch and we reminisce about the days gone by. It was a fascinating career with unforgettable challenges. I wish I were still capable of climbing the steep gangways to visit some of the captains I befriended over the years. Alas, I simply have to rely on Martha to extend my greetings to them.

We shall be spending Christmas in San Francisco with my son Rodney and his family and I'm looking forward to hugging my two grandsons for the very first time. Rodney is a respected architect and I am really proud of his accomplishments. He is happily married to a gorgeous-looking school teacher.

Now for the biggest blessing of the year. Martina is expecting our child, who will be born next spring. I will be sixty-two years old when the baby arrives but age will not deter me from performing the duties of a loving and caring father.

As the new year draws near, we are being told that another war with Iraq is inevitable. The tragedy of September 11, 2001, has made America more concerned about the evil nature of terrorism. However, having been involved in Vietnam, I think that there must be another alternative to the horrors of war. War is sinful. War makes killers of young men and women who develop emotional scars that they would have to be burdened with for the rest of their lives. Please join me in my prayers for peace on earth.

Well, dear friends, this is my Christmas letter for 2002. You are probably familiar with a famous Christmas letter to a little girl called Virginia who wanted to prove to her friends that Santa Claus existed. Like the author in that letter, I say "Yes, Virginia, there is a Santa Claus." There are also angels and Jewish leprechauns.

May you and yours have the best holiday season ever.

Affectionately,
Jim Blackburn